I0780024

SANA' WATTS

The Detour

A novel by Sana' Watts

Copyright © 2025 by Sana Watts
Published by Forget Me Not Romances, an imprint of Winged Publications

Editor: Cynthia Hickey
Book Design by Forget Me Not Romances

All rights reserved. No part of this publication may be reproduced, stored in a retrieval system, or transmitted in any form or by any means—electronic, mechanical, photocopying, recording, or otherwise—without the prior written permission of
the publisher. The only exception is brief quotations in printed reviews. Piracy is illegal. Thank you for respecting the hard work of this author.

This book is a work of fiction. Names, characters, Places, incidents, and dialogues are either products of the author's imagination or used fictitiously.
Any resemblance to actual persons, living or dead, or events is coincidental. Scripture quotations from The Authorized (King James) Version.

Fiction and Literature: Inspirational
Christian Romance

Disclaimer: Contains mild adult situations and the consequences

ISBN-13: 978-1-965352-77-9

Dedication

This is for 17-year-old Sana' who first thought of this story for her grade 12 Writer's Craft Class. It's been just over a decade in the making, but God brought us here for our joy and His glory.

Acknowledgements

First, I'd like to thank you, the one reading these words. Thank you for taking the chance on my debut novel. Whether it was the cover, the book description, the early low price, or anything else - I'm grateful for you reading this story. I hope it was worthy of your time.

Next, I'd like to thank Cynthia who saw something in this story and chose to invest her time, energy, and creativity into publishing this novel. Thank you Diane for challenging me to grow as a writer to see this story be at its technical best.

Moreover, I have to shoutout the original Hawt Messies. You have all been such an incredible community to me these past 3ish years. I hope and pray that every Christian woman gets to experience the kind of sisterhood I've been blessed with in you.

To my momma. Thank you for being my alpha reader, encourager and prayer warrior. You never gave up on this series being published, even when I did. You held faith and hope for me. Your prayers have been answered!

To my covenant bae, Desmond. I stand by the statement that you are the second greatest gift God gave to me, the gospel being first. Through you, I experience what gospel love stories are meant to be. You've set the highest standard that all my male protagonists must live up to. Thank you for listening to me, supporting me, holding me and bragging about me. I love you.

And to the Alpha and Omega, Yahweh my Triune God. This story was created by, through and for You. To You alone be the glory, amen.

Prologue

"Ruthia, don't forget to call your dad," Shane reminded me as we pulled out of the school parking lot, just having finished with our on-campus Bible Study.

I sighed. "I know you're right, but needing to check in with my parents so often makes me feel like I'm twelve instead of twenty."

"Valid feelings. Perhaps someday you'll discuss this with them. But, for now, still make that call."

With another dramatic sigh that made him chuckle, I pulled out my phone and swiped to call my dad. "Hi, Daddy."

"Hey, honey, what's going on with your plans?" he asked, but I heard movement in the background.

"I'm coming home right now. I'll arrive in around ten minutes. A friend's bringing me home." I told him, inwardly cringing at the lie I just added to all the ones I've told in the last year. I resent concealing my relationship, but a romance with the son of the church schism's instigator would be a problem.

"Okay, but your mother and I won't be there. The church blessed us with a weekend away in Niagara, and we're packing now. I imagine that we'll leave right before you get home."

"That's great!" I answered with enthusiasm. "You two have fun now."

"Thanks, hon, see you Sunday night. Love you!"

"Love you too, bye!" I hung up the phone and relayed the news to Shane. We chatted a bit about Niagara Falls and what it would be like to visit there until we reached the house. I knew they had gone; their car was missing from the driveway.

This is our usual moment for a good-night kiss before I go indoors. But it occurred to me that tonight could be different.

"Want to come inside and hang out?" I asked him. When he didn't answer right away, I got a lot more nervous. "I mean, you don't have to. I just figured that we never got to debrief the Bible study and -"

"Thia, chill." He gently interrupted me. "You don't have to convince me to spend more time with you. I am always happy to delay our goodbyes. I was just surprised at the invitation, okay?"

At his words, I am calmed. "Okay."

When we get inside, the nerves return, but for a different reason. Our clandestine relationship meant we'd never been to my home. He lived on his own near campus, so we just spent time there. I was suddenly hyper-aware of all the flaws in my home.

"Get comfortable in the living room. It's just on the left. I'll head to the kitchen and grab us something to drink. What would you like?"

"Water is good."

"Gotcha. I'll be right back."

I make quick work of pouring myself a glass of orange juice and Shane one of water. Returning, I found Shane examining wall photos.

"You were an adorable baby." He told me and I blushed - again.

"The glorious days when I was light-skinned." I joked and went to sit on the couch, but he grabbed my hand to stop me.

"Hey, not so fast." I rarely heard his voice be this serious. "None of that colorism crap. Your dark brown skin is beautiful to me. I wouldn't change a thing.

"I hear you, and I thank you.," I gave him a quick kiss on the cheek. "Shall we sit?"

He nodded, and I headed over to our new sectional, placing our glasses in the cup holders. Shane spread out horizontally with his legs open, and I smiled. This was our favourite cuddling position. I sat in between his legs, leaning against his chest, his head resting on top of mine.

I could stay here forever with no complaints.

"Alright, so that Bible study was fire," I said after a moment.

"I thought that discussion on 2 Corinthians 4 was powerful. The text itself, with no commentary, hits hard, to be honest," he was saying. I nodded in agreement.

"Right! That entire part about struggling but still going is one of my favourites. It was one of the first scriptures I memorized because of the song 'Trading My Sorrows'. Do you remember it?"

"Yeah." he responded with a laugh and sang, "I

am pressed but not crushed, persecuted, not abandoned, struck down but not destroyed..."

"... I am blessed beyond the curse, for his promise shall endure and his joy's going to be my strength." I finished, slightly off-key.

"No cap, those are bars. We didn't realize as kids how powerful those lyrics were."

"For real! Those verses have been such an anchor for me amid and when recovering from anxiety attacks. Knowing that what I'm going through doesn't have the final say in my destiny and that God will never abandon me has helped me so much. I know what it's like to be struck down in the attacks I have. But God has always seen me through to the other side."

He nodded. "You know, it's amazing how encouraging and relevant to today the Bible is, considering someone penned those words thousands of years ago. Would you like to share more about the anxiety you struggle with? It's not something that you often bring up."

He's right. This topic surfaced only a few times during our relationship. "A sense of impending disaster," I began, searching for the right explanation. "That's what it feels like. The uncertainty of the future is like a physical weight on my chest. Most of the time, I can ignore it or put my restless energy elsewhere, but when I can't - that weight gets so heavy that it's hard to breathe. My heart races more, my breathing gets shallow, and then I'm in an anxiety attack. Even talking about it brings the anxiety to the forefront of my mind."

"Thanks for that description. I appreciate you

trusting me with all of that. Do you remember when this first started?"

"Hmm., I think I've struggled with this since I was a kid, but I didn't have the language for it. For example, whenever I had something for school or any competitive activity, there would be anxiety about what would happen if it didn't go well. I know it's normal to feel nervous and get a rush of adrenaline when something significant is happening, but this is more than that. It would feel like I had no control over my body and that somehow, I was going to fail, and failure is dangerous, because if I fail - will people still care about me? My default answer to that question is no, and that's kind of where the root of my anxiety is; that I'm always on the cusp of being rejected and alone."

"That's a lot, Thia, and that sounds really hard."

"It was, and it still is, to be honest. God's work through therapy has helped me gain self-awareness, allowing me to articulate what I shared. But the anxiety isn't gone, you know? It's just managed through inner work and taking my medications."

"Hmm. Does that worry you? Like, do you think it will ever go away?"

"Honestly, I'm not sure. And it's hard as a Christian struggling with this because often it's looked at as a failure of faith, like I'm just not working hard enough to trust God, and that's why I'm feeling the way I do. Or, if I was really a Christian, God would just heal me."

"Those things are not even Biblical though! I'm legit heated that people have said that to you!" His voice rose, and his hands moved around angrily. I took one of them in my own and squeezed it gently.

"Babe, it's okay. Those things hurt, but I'm used to them by now." I tried to assure him, but I could feel his head shaking.

"No, it's not okay and not just because people said these things to you, someone I care about. But it's just Biblically illiterate! As you were sharing, it made me think of another passage in 2 Corinthians in chapter 12. In it, Paul talks about having something painful in his life, a thorn in his side, that he's asked God to take away three times! And God says no, but to trust that His grace is enough to keep going. Maybe that's what anxiety is in your life. Maybe it's a thorn that God is allowing in your life for some other purpose. Only God knows, and people shouldn't presume to know what God's will for your life is."

"I forgot about that scripture. That's a good one to keep in mind, especially since it rings true. His grace has been enough for me. Thank you for sharing that with me." I replied, beginning to cry. "I don't even know why I'm crying, it's stupid -"

"No, it's not, Thia. This is intense stuff. I think your feelings are super valid and honestly, the way you've persevered through all the anxiety you experience makes you one of the strongest people I know. For real."

Those words just made me cry more. He held me tightly as the tears came and offered me the end of his sleeve as a tissue.

"I appreciate your words and your passion for God's Word." I eventually said once the tears abated.

In response, he leaned his head forward and kissed my cheek. Smiling, I turned around to face him, my legs tucked under me. I placed my hands on his shoulders and gave him a kiss, to really show him my appreciation.

I reopened my eyes to find resolve in his dark brown eyes. "Ruthia, I love you." I stared at him in shock. He never said that before. I had hoped this was the case - since I'd been feeling the same way for months- but it still somehow felt hard to believe; like it was too good to be true. "You don't have to say it back. I just wanted you to know where I'm at."

He misinterpreted my silence.

"No, I mean, gah. I'm crap at this." I take a deep breath. "I love you too."

Watching my words hit him in real time is something I'm unlikely to forget. It's like they got brighter, like I'd lit something within him.

I'm unsure of who initiated the kiss, but it felt different from the others. Like, our professed love had added a weight to it, infusing it with meaning.

We stayed that way, losing track of time. As he deepened the kiss, his hands went just above the waistband of my jeans. I leaned into him so that we were chest to chest. His body started to slide lower until we were almost horizontal. I barely registered the position that we were in; I wasn't thinking. I was feeling, feeling so cared for by him and so thankful for our relationship.

We broke apart for a moment and then I realized that I was actually on top of him. I have no clue how it happened, and I didn't care.

Only he mattered.

I felt his fingers tugging at my sweater. and I pulled back from the kiss to lift it over my head.

throwing it beside us on the floor. Shane did the same thing and then our bare skin was touching.

It was the first time he would've seen me in a bra, and his eyes widened, showing something akin to awe. His fingers grazed the part of my breast that wasn't contained. I shivered at the touch. It felt better than I could've imagined.

I laid my head on his bare chest. I could hear his heart beating fast and knew that mine was probably beating at the same rate. Tilting my head up, I saw a raw yearning in his eyes, as if I were the only glass of water to quench his thirst.

It undid me.

I kissed him with a desire of my own. As we kissed, I noticed a bulge underneath me. Usually, this is where I would break us apart, and we'd move away from each other guiltily. But I didn't want to do that this time; I didn't want to hold my love for him back, not anymore.

The evidence of his arousal opened the door to a need I didn't even realize I had. It just felt so good. I shifted my body, trying to ease the ache I felt. My pulse was beating in my core and every touch felt intimate. Yet there was a frenetic urgency to appease the need that was growing by the second. As I moved against him faster, he stopped us by tenderly lifting me off of him and then getting up from the couch.

Displeasure filled every part of me.

"Why did you stop us?" I asked, breathless.

"Thia, trust me, I want us to keep going. But if you kept doing that, I was going to finish quickly, but you might not have. I also wanted to make sure that you actually want this."

I let out a frustrated sigh. He was unfailingly courteous.

"Yes, I want this. More than I even thought possible."

"I don't have anything." He told me.

"You don't have to worry about that. I've been on the pill for a while now." At this admission, he looked surprised and a little suspicious, so I rushed to explain. "It helps with my period cramps." He nodded his head in understanding, looking relieved. "Anyhow, I'm not worried about diseases, since we're both virgins." It's only after I say the words that I realize the assumption I'd made. "Wait, I realized we've never talked about this. Are you…"

"Yes, I am. I've been saving myself for my wife, but I can't imagine loving anyone as much as I love you."

My heart melted, and my core responded in kind, becoming even more warm. "I could tell you how much I love you back, or I could just show you."

I got up and held out my hand to help him stand, then I led him to my room. I opened the door and its neatness relieved me.

The rest of the night is an awkward type of wonderful. Our touches are a mix of hesitant and confident, savoring each other but moving with an urgency to be as close as we can get. We don't just have sex, we make love - and I understand what that phrase means. That our love has had its most tangible expression in our bodies uniting with each other.

As I lay tucked against his body, my head on his bare chest, I try my best to quiet the still small voice telling me I've made a grievous mistake - and there will be consequences.

Chapter 1

At 5:45 AM, I sit here, apprehensive about the test results. Through blurry, tear-filled vision, two lines are visible.

I am pregnant.

No.

No.

I shake the stick. Is it broken? Maybe it malfunctioned? These things weren't that accurate, right? I reach for the box and read those big bold letters: 99% accuracy.

Damn it. What am I going to do? I try to take calming breaths.

This is so unbelievable. Like, yes. We messed up. But we did everything right afterwards! Following our time of intimacy, we confessed to our campus ministry leaders and implemented new boundaries. We've barely even kissed since then, and we were even talking about telling our parents about us.

Oh.

My.

Lord.

My parents.

How would they take the news?

My chest tightens, and I have to fight to breathe. My heart beats faster and faster as all the implications of this pregnancy hit me. I try to take deep breaths, but it's no use. I curl up into a ball on my bathroom floor and cry, waiting out the panic attack until it is done.

Once my body calms down, I think about my next steps.

I need to tell Shane. It would be so much easier to decide everything and tell our parents together. I dry my eyes with some toilet paper and grab my phone, calling him before I lose my nerve.

"Hey, Thia." I instantly smile. His voice and his greeting are so familiar that everything else happening doesn't seem so bad.

"Hey, there's something important I have to tell you. Meet me at Timmy's in fifteen minutes?"

"Sure, I'll see you there, babe. Love you." My smile grows so large that he could probably hear it in my voice.

"I love you too."

Tim Hortons was only a five-minute walk from my house, so I take time to freshen up. It's my routine to jog in the mornings, which is why my parents didn't even stir when I'd left the house at 5:15 to run to the nearest Shoppers Drug Mart and pick up a pregnancy test.

I glance at myself in the mirror, my eyes involuntarily moving to my stomach. I put my hand on it and then the realization hits me. Inside of me is life.

It was time for me to meet Shane.

I walk over to Tim Hortons and enter the establishment to see that Shane is waiting for me there at a table. Orange juice and a cinnamon roll laid out for me. I smile at my favourite order from Timmy's and allow him to hug me.

"So, what's all of this for?"

"The last early morning meeting you called here was when you got the practicum you wanted! I figured this was another celebration." He looks so excited.

Damn, how am I going to break it to him? How do I tell him he will become a father in under 8 months? I never expected that telling Shane would be so hard. I close my eyes, afraid of how he'll look when he hears the news.

"I'm pregnant." I push the two words out with difficulty, and the weight of this reality lifts off my shoulders. It feels better not having to deal with it all on my own. But then I am aware of his silence. Every quiet second seems like a century has gone by. I open my eyes to see his stunned face.

I try to read him through his eyes, but when I look into them, they're blank. I actually recognize this look as his "calculating face". Whenever he is trying to figure out a problem, he takes on the look and then he gets the answer. When it passes, I look at him expectantly.

This was when he was going to say, 'We'll get through this. I love you and will stand by your side. This baby will receive unparalleled parental affection.'

"I... can't," he finally says.

"Pardon me?" I didn't think I'd heard him

properly.

"I'm sorry, Ruthia, but this… no."

"What do you mean by no?"

His eyes meet mine, softening his facial expression and showing love, briefly making me think he would confess it was all a joke and revert to the familiar Shane I knew. But then his eyes trail down to my stomach and a look of horror overcomes his features. It's so abrupt and so distorted that I flinch.

"I'm sorry Thia, but this situation is too much. I can't… this will not work." He gets up from his seat and rushes to the exit.

"Which one won't work, the baby or us?"

I look at him pleadingly, his face blurry through my tears.

"Either, both. Whatever."

I'm driven to chase him, unleash my fury, obliterate our history. I want to undo what we'd done; the thing that had messed everything up in the first place: having sex.

I brush away my tears with the edges of my sleeve and sit down at the table. How could he do this to me? Where was the Shane that would say that he loved me? That he'd always be there for me, no matter what? When had this monster replaced him, the one who left me only moments ago? Fourteen months of my life thrown away. I feel my heart harden and crack. All I feel is pain and anger.

And it is because of this damn baby.

If I wasn't pregnant, this never would've happened. I check my phone, and it reads 6:30. At this moment, I would be taking a shower after my run. My parents would still be asleep, so Shane would pick me up and be my ride to campus.

Everything was off.

I would eliminate this baby before it could inflict more damage on my life. It wasn't innocent. Because of it, I'd lost the man I loved. How else would it ruin me? I didn't want to find out.

Forget classes today. Dealing with this is much more important. I get up from my chair so quickly that I jostle the food for me on the table. A part of me wants to throw it out, but my parents have instilled in me that I should never throw out food, and these were my favorites. Instead, I take 5 dollars out of my pocket — change from the pregnancy test — grab the food and walk up to the counter, cutting in front of waiting customers.

I give the cashier my money to pay.

"But miss, they're already paid for!" she calls out to me, but I ignore her and push my way through the doors of the restaurant. I still hear her voice and those of the angry customers, but I don't care.

I did what I had to do. My happiness will not stem from Shane. I was on my own. By paying for this food myself, I was taking my first steps toward my independence.

Chapter 2

As soon as I reach home, I head to my room and go to the top left drawer of my dresser, where I keep everything having to do with Shane and me. All the notes, photos, borrowed clothes, gifts, printed out conversations, the USB with some of our recorded Zoom calls, and all the songs, poems, and diary entries relating to us are in that drawer.

Angrily, I grab an empty box in my closet and dump everything in it. I put the cover on it, grab my purse, and drop my cell phone into it. As I rush out of my room, I slip on the edge of my carpet and the box falls from my hands, its contents strewn all over my floor.

Wonderful.

I crouch down to grab them, intending to just shove them all back in the box, but my heart catches when I see everything laid out. I know I shouldn't, but I opt to sit down on the floor and really go through the things that fell. Maybe I'll be able to find out what went wrong, what I missed that led me to today.

First, I see pictures we'd taken together. Shane and I were in a photo booth, laughing, making silly faces, and kissing. I gulp and see more pictures. The photos, posed and candid, show us both thrilled to be with each other. And then I come across pictures of us as kids. I chuckle at the memories. There we are at Wild Water Kingdom with the rest of the children's ministry, both 8 years old. And there we are around a square table playing dominoes against another double at 11 years old. We intently focus on our dominoes but steal glances at one another.

Finally, I get to the end of the pictures to see fourteen different folders. One for each month of our relationship.

Out of curiosity, I pick up Month One. As I scan through the conversations, I notice how often we were always laughing. The LOLs take up maybe a third of our conversations, with good reason. I laugh, just rereading them. We're hilarious together. Our wit is too much. And then I see a part that's highlighted. I flip back a bit to see what led up to it.

Shane Reid
5:15 pm
Hey ☺
Ruthia Walkins
5:15 pm
Hey ☺
Shane Reid
5:16 pm
☺
Ruthia Walkins
5:16 pm
☺
Shane Reid

5:17 pm

I can continue this indefinitely, Ruthia. I don't think I'll ever be able to stop smiling.

Oh crap, why do I always just blurt these things out?

Ruthia Walkins

5:18 pm

LOOL. Relax, it doesn't make me like you any less. :P

I promise ☺

If anything, it makes me like you more because you're not filtering yourself around me. You're being beautifully (instead of brutally) honest.

And there's my #NoFilter statement of the day. XP

Shane Reid

5:20 pm

Thank you. ☺ We should each share a #NoFilter statement at least once a day. Deal?

Ruthia Walkins

5:20 pm

Deal. * reaches out a hand for a handshake*

I smile at this. We maintain a daily practice of No Filter Statements. Or, at least, we did. I had forgotten how it had gotten started. I really enjoyed reading this.

Shane Reid

5:21 pm

shakes hand… but doesn't let go ;)

Ruthia Walkins

5:21 pm

Ready for a secret? She doesn't want you to ;D

Oh! Sorry, random switch in the conversation, but I just saw a link to this site that's supposed to be great for couples.

Shane Reid

5:22 pm

I'm 99% certain that was divine intervention; what was it for?

Ruthia Walkins

5:22 pm

Something about love languages. There's a quiz. Want to each do it and see what the results are? And I just took in what you said, Amen ☺ #JesusAtTheCenter #Always

Shane Reid

5:23 pm

Agreed. ☺ and sure! Send the link?

Ruthia Walkins

5:23 pm

Here it is: http://www.5lovelanguages.com/

Ruthia Walkins

5:24 pm

Oh. Choose single when you get there.

Shane Reid

5:24 pm

Breaking up with me already, eh? :P

Ruthia Walkins

5:24 pm

LOL. Would you rather be married? XP

Shane Reid

5:25 pm

Now you're proposing? I don't know if I can handle all the mood swings, Thia. :P #MakeUpYourMind

Ruthia Walkins

5:25 pm

LOOOL. Well, if you can't handle my moodiness, then I don't think you're the right man for me.

Hmph. *lifts nose in a prissy fashion and walks away*

Shane Reid

5:26 pm

WAIT. Don't leave me. *runs after you and takes you into my arms.*

I can change! I promise.

Ruthia Walkins

5:26 pm

Fine. You can be back in my life, but only as a friend. :P

Shane Reid

5:27 pm

And that was the end of the relationship of...

Ruthia Walkins

5:27 pm

Frank and Bernice.

high five

I laugh out loud after reading that. It was something we'd been doing since we were kids. We'd either overact for comedic effect or invent stories mid-conversation.

Shane Reid

5:28 pm

high five Have you finished the questionnaire yet?

Ruthia Walkins

5:29 pm

From time. Ready to share the results?

Shane Reid

5:29 pm
In 3...
Ruthia Walkins
5:29 pm
2 ....
Shane Reid
5:30 pm
1! Ladies First ☺ ;)
Ruthia Walkins
5:31 pm
My top three are: Words of Affirmation, Quality Time and Receiving Gifts in that order ☺ I feel like they sum me up perfectly! XD Yours?
Shane Reid
5:31 pm
Interesting. My top 3 are physical touch, quality time, and words of affirmation in that order. They really are scarily accurate, eh?
Ruthia Walkins
5:31 pm
Omg! Out of our top three, we have two in common! #AlmostPerfectMatch ☺
Shane Reid
5:33 pm
I've always thought that when God made man, He formed our personalities, our likes and dislikes, and would choose someone for us that would complement them nicely. These results seem like confirmation of that.
Ruthia Walkins
5:35 pm
I think you're right. It's one reason we should always trust God, you know? God is the ultimate

matchmaker because He knows every part of us and sees which two people could actually make One, instead of a lot of relationships today where they don't unify. They're just two people lumped together.

Oh! Time for dinner. ☺ Ttyl Shane! *kiss on the cheek*

Ruthia Walkins is offline.

Then there's a note I made in the margins.

Remember, his first love language is physical touch. That means giving him little touches here and there to comfort him and assurance. Sigh. This is making me so uncomfortable. Not because I don't want to touch Shane—just the opposite. I love touching him, so I have to be careful that in speaking his primary love language, I don't over-tempt myself—or drive the risk of tempting him. Oh dear. Now I'm feeling awkward. Guess I know what will definitely be on my prayer list tonight. For me to know how to touch Shane. And that sounds even worse! Oh, Lord.

Even at the very beginning of our relationship, I was smitten. Here I was trying to figure out how to speak his love language, for goodness' sake! How did it all go so wrong?

I drop the folders in the box and then gather the USBs. Most are mixtapes he'd made for me. Some with love songs, but most were gospel mixes. He always tried to find underground artists and surprise me with delightful music. I grab one at random and stick it in my laptop, ready to hear some music play.

But there is none, just silence until... "Hello!" I

hear my voice ring throughout the room. I sound so happy, practically singing the words. Shane laughs.

"Someone seems to be in a rather good mood," Shane says, teasing her.

"Well, I am. The kids were amazing today, Shane." Ruthia replies with a content sigh. "Oh, FYI, there's just so much I want to process from today that I'm recording it to listen to later."

"No probs. Tell me all about tonight." Shane says.

"The kids were just ... gosh. I can't explain it. They were so well-behaved, but not robots either! We could have fun! We played freeze dance, and I got them to do the sprinkler with me." She giggles. "They were so adorable. And then during the lesson, those precious 4- and 5-year-olds listened so well. They clearly grasped the lesson's key takeaway. One little boy, Jaden, even asked to pray. He melted my heart with his prayer. He's going to be a pastor when he's older. I just know it." She takes a breath, and Shane speaks.

"Oh? Is that so? How would you know?" He teases her.

She laughs. "I live with one, don't I? It's like I have radar for these things." She jokes. I laugh along with Shane.

"And then what happened?" He asks her.

"When this little girl was being picked up, she hugged me around my legs and told me she loved me."

"Well, then, that little girl is very intelligent, then." Shane says matter-of-factly.

"Oh? And why do you say that?"

"Because you are very loveable. Just ask your parents." I roll my eyes at this as USB Ruthia snorts.

"Oh goodness, now look what you've done!" she says, pretending to sound angry but losing it in her giggles.

"Me? How have I erred you, my lady?" Shane says innocently, feigning a British accent. I can practically see his smile.

"Oh, Sir Shane, in your outward and outlandish display of humor, you have ruined me. The snort," she paused dramatically, her British accent laughable, *"will forever tarnish my reputation."*

And then we're both laughing uncontrollably on the phone. Listening to it now, I laugh along with them. Their laughter is so contagious that I can't help it.

Pure joy radiated from us.

I shake my head and focus on the conversation. We've finally finished laughing.

"But on a serious note, Shane, today taught me something." She says, trying to get control of her voice.

"Me too. I learned that your snorting adds years to my life through laughter." Shane jokes, and she giggles once more.

"No! Stop it!" she protests, giggling. *"I have something important to say."*

"Okay, I'll be well-behaved. What's on your mind?" Shane says calmly.

"Thank you, hon. I realized today how much a child reflect their parents. This evening, instead of just

one parent doing the picking up, I saw a lot of parents in a couple picking them up, and it hit me how children are truly a mix of their parents. Like Soraya, that little girl I love? I would never have realized she had her dad's nose if he hadn't picked her up. It really hit me that choosing a guy to be with is serious. This search extends beyond preferences; you desire someone worthy of parental status."

There's silence as I process her words. Shane and I both.

"Deep Thia, beyond deep. I'm not talking like the deep end of a swimming pool here, but like when you go too far out into the ocean. It's funny because I've never heard that said before. I've heard no sermons on relationships and waiting for your future spouse to explore that concept. Your search is for a significant other who can excel as both a life companion and a parent."

"Exactly. This reveals exciting possibilities. Because, instead of having a set of characteristics that you want to find in a spouse, you think of what you want your children to inherit."

Shane instantly replies. "That's so true. I feel like our peers need to hear this message. If the guys I know had to consider, they might not date these girls thinking, 'This could be the mother of my children'."

"Right?! Same with so many girls I know. Like, honestly. You want the bad boy who low rides his pants and smokes weed, that's great. Will he be able to teach your son chivalry? Do you see him tucking in your little girl at night? It puts things in perspective. People treat dating like... like..."

"Like a sport!" He supplies the right word, and

she laughs.

"Yes! That's perfection. They just get into a million relationships without thinking. Dating, it's not just a pastime. It's being with somebody who–"

"–you might spend the rest of your life with." Shane finishes for her.

"And who will end up being a parent alongside you, passing down genes to the children." She adds.

"Oh no. My kids might inherit my weirdly shaped ears." Shane blurts out.

She laughs. "Please, your ears are not weird." She says as if he's being ridiculous.

"Thia, they are disproportionate to my head."

"Disproportionate or not, I think they're cute. My kids now, jeez, they'll inherit my burping. Now that's a problem."

Shane laughs. "To whom? Your mother?" he laughs again.

"You haven't seen her face when I let it rip. She looks horrified at the same time." She says through her laughter.

"Actually, I have seen it, remember..." He says teasingly.

"Oh, no. You are not bringing that up." She says, trying to be stern but failing.

I laugh out loud as I remember what event they're talking about.

"It was priceless. We're all enjoying the banquet honoring the visiting pastor. .... Your mom gives the closing speech and then gives you a shout-out for helping to plan part of the event. .... You look beautiful in that purple dress, holding a wine glass of ginger ale. You open your mouth to thank your mother

and .... and the committee for a chance to serve and then. And then....." Shane can barely get out the rest of the story. He's laughing too hard. Ruthia isn't even attempting to stop him because she's dying of laughter as well.

He finally regains some breath. "And then you burp, this amazingly loud truck driver burp that shocks the whole room!"

"It's not funny!" Ruthia protests, while laughing.

"Oh, the look on your mother's face! There should've been a camera!" Stereo Shane is dying.

"Oh, that was so mortifying," Ruthia says, the laughter draining from her voice.

"Thia, I thought it was cute."

"Cute. How is burping like a truck driver cute?" she asks dubiously.

"Because, when you burp, it's like you're showing who you really are."

Silence.

"Did you just call me a belch? An eructation?" All the amusement is gone.

"No, well, yes. But, okay. Thia, listen."

"I'm listening."

"You are so beautiful and classy, right? Elegant and intelligent. That's your public persona."

"Flattery, eh? Good start." She teases.

"But there's this whole other side to you that most people don't get to see. Someone who's kind of crazy but entertaining, who drops wisdom intertwined with humor. I'm honored to know someone who shows such childlike enthusiasm. And when you burp, it's like those two different sides of you meeting at the same intersection. That's... that's what I meant."

How could he consistently say the right thing, yet bail when I needed him the most?

"Wow. Oh, my goodness. I just realized something." Ruthia says, breathless.

"What?"

"Oh, you don't want to know." She teases.

"Try me." Shane teases back.

"Well, as the day progresses... nah. You can't handle this."

Shane laughs. "Yes, yes I can!"

"Okay," she says, purposefully sounding doubtful. I laugh. She really is too much sometimes. "As time goes by during the day ... the sky ... gets ... darker. Boom." She says dramatically.

Shane and I both laugh. "Well done, Sherlock."

She laughs too. "Thank you."

"But legit. What did you realize?" He asks her. She scoffs.

"Adorable. You genuinely believed I'd reveal that. Anyway, it's almost midnight and I should go to bed." Her voice then sounds tired.

"Wait, what? Already? It's Friday night!" Shane protests.

"I have that women's prayer breakfast tomorrow morning, remember? And I'm supposed to be doing a little exhortation during it."

"I wish I could be there, Thia. I love hearing you speak."

"I would be absolutely delighted if you could attend. But there's this slight biological problem. You're without a uterus." She jokes.

"Oh drat. How had I missed that little detail?" he jokes back, and she giggles. "Do you think

someone will record you speaking?"

"Maybe my mother. Here's hoping that I don't burp again." She giggles. "You know how I get worse with orange juice."

"I will pray over the breakfast. You'll be amazing up there, babe."

"Thank you, hon." She replies, tired.

"And babe?"

"Mhm?" she mumbles. Her fatigue is clear now. "Even if your children inherit only a little of your wisdom, wit, beauty, and intelligence, burping won't bother them. They're going to be amazing, just like their mother. Thank you for staying on until midnight for me. Happy six-month anniversary." Shane says the words slowly.

I can practically see myself sitting up, rubbing my eyes, and wondering if I just heard him correctly. What I hadn't told him was that I just realized that he might love me and that I was loving him back.

"Happy anniversary to you too, Shane. Your words inspire flight, yet firm my footing unlike ever before. You will be an amazing father one day, ears and all."

The love in my voice.

I can't bear it.

The warmth, joy, and love radiating through it was too much for me.

I get up to shut the audio off. I don't want to hear anymore. Unceremoniously, I drop all the USBs in the box and move on to the last thing: the journal I kept with Shane's name on it.

I browse entries until locating one following

Valentine's Day.

Okay, Diary, should I be worried? About Shane and me? Is something wrong with us? Because I feel like we're too perfect.

I mean, we've been together for nine months now. And I don't think we've ever had a legit argument. Yeah, we have playful debates sometimes, but they're not serious stuff. I've been searching our conversations, and I can only find the time when he got the worst of one of my panic attacks. That was the one time.

Isn't that wrong? Couples are supposed to have fights and argue and get on each other's nerves. It's through working through those things that they get closer! Suppose this relationship fails because of a lack of conflict.

I know, I know. I'm overthinking this, right? I mean, we're great. Shane and I ... we're better than great. I don't think I've ever been this happy, and he brings me closer to God. The conversations we have, the way he lives as a genuine man of God.... It just makes me love him more.

There, I said it. I love Shane. I've been thinking about it for a while now, and I think he might love me too, but I will say nothing until he does. How mortifying would that be? And from all the movies I watched, saying I love you too early to a guy scares them off.

I'll keep this private, for now.

But gosh, I really love him, diary. Shane Nathaniel Reid. Mrs. Ruthia Reid.

Sounds good, right? But that's why I'm so worried! How do I know we can actually make it if we have developed no resiliency through arguments and stuff? I don't know if I could bear us breaking up.

No, that's a lie. I don't need Shane. I could live without him.

I just don't want to.

I daily want him, God willing, in my life.

I sound crazy, don't I? Okay, you know what? I'm going to list the things that annoy me about him. I might uncover something to dispute. XD

Okay. Hmmm. Oh! I have one. He bites his nails when he's nervous. That's gross. Well, except I bite my nails too. His trigger is nervousness; mine is laziness.

Damn. That doesn't work. Oh! His leg. Whenever he sits down somewhere, it shakes incessantly. That can be super distracting. But then, as soon as I lay my hand on his leg, it stops. And then I feel so close to him, and he smiles at me like I'm the answer to all his problems because I spoke his love language....

So, great. That doesn't work either.

I honestly can't think of anything else. I'm sure there are annoying things he does, it's just that I love him, and I choose him, regardless of those things. So, they don't matter to me.

Maybe, that's the resiliency? Maybe it's not just having disagreements and stuff. Maybe, it's in knowing what things annoy you and not caring about them because you choose the person, no matter what.

Well, it's been a pleasure talking this out with you.

Until the next entry,

(Hopefully one day) Mrs. Ruthia Reid.

I sigh as I finish reading that entry and place the journal in the box with everything else. I don't need to see anymore. There were no signs pointing to what happened today. No red flags that I can deduce. My shock feels validated, and my resolve strengthened. Past Ruthia knew she could live without him. And she was right. I was right. I will move forward in my life without him in it.

One day, he'll be only a somewhat sad memory.

With that thought, I leave the house again, carrying the box with me. Two buses and one block of walking later, I am at Shane's apartment building. I enter using the code, then walk to his ground-floor apartment. I knock on his door and wait for him to answer. He does and is about to close the door in my face—rude—when he notices the box in my hands.

"What's that?" he asks me.

"A box filled with baby naming books, nursery catalogues and old baby toys. I figured we would start planning it all together now." I say sarcastically and scoff. "It actually has everything to do with us. I didn't want any of it anymore, so here you go." I tell him.

"And what am I supposed to do with this?" he asks me.

"Do I look like I care about what you do anymore?" I reply.

Shane looks shocked at my reply. His shocked face is the last thing I see before dropping the box at his feet and walking away.

Chapter 3

I try to appear calm as I walk away from Shane, but on the inside, my heart is all in shambles. At least I can check Shane off my list for those I'm letting go of, and now it's this baby. Forget about the ethics, and how it goes against everything I believe in, I just can't do this anymore. Once I let go of it, I can restart for real; and not mess up this time.

I grab a bus to the Civic Centre that houses my favorite library, a daycare downstairs and toward the back: an abortion clinic.

I'll get the job done and then pick out some books to get my mind off of it. I'd have a restful day at the library.

But the bus ride is long, and as I lean my head against the window, I see an adorable couple walking together on the sidewalk, swinging their arms, fingers interlocked, bright smiles on their faces.

I don't even realize I am crying until I see a spot on my track pants and notice a teardrop.

I dig around in my purse and find a crumpled-up tissue. It is almost symbolic, crumpled up and unable to be perfect again; all mangled and ripped. This tissue is like a mirror.

This makes me weep.

As soon as the bus reaches the Civic Centre, I head straight toward the washroom and cry it out in a stall. Silent tears, I assume because doors open and close; I hear the toilets flush; the water running as people wash their hands, girls laughing together, and no one seems to hear me.

Or maybe they just don't care.

Honestly, no one really cares, and you have to look out for yourself because when you really believe that someone does, they let you down. Better you remained uncaring from the outset.

And from now on, that's what I was going to do.

With a big bundle of toilet paper in my right hand, I dry my tears and then flush it all away. I exit the stall, wash my face at the sink, and rinse out my eyes.

After doing all of that, I feel better. Crying it all out was the catharsis I needed.

Next stop on the journey of recovery: Abortion clinic.

I look at the sign above the two different stairwells and it shows that the 'Women's Health Clinic' is on the bottom floor past various activity rooms at the back of the centre. This makes perfect sense because who would want to see girls waiting to kill their unborn babies right beside the library?

Yeah, I don't see any volunteers raising their hands either.

And yet, those three words… they bring me hope; a solution to my problem. Those three words assure me I won't have to deal with all of this anymore.

My heart thumps with every footstep I make, I race down the stairs and look up for further directions to the clinic. Speed walking, I'm getting hyped and excited.

And then I slip on something and fall straight on my back. I'm just so thankful that my head hits the carpet.

"Sorry."

I move my head in the small voice's direction to see a young girl with a caramel complexion and dark brown hair pulled back into pigtails. She looks to be about 3 years old.

"That's my ball."

I see a bright green bouncy ball just below, centimeters away. I get up, grab the ball and walk toward her. She looks scared until I crouch and hand it to her.

"Don't worry, honey. I'm fine."

That awards me a brilliant smile from her, and I smile back.

"My name is Cynthia!"

"No, no, it's not!" I infuse my voice with shock.

She giggles and nods. "It is! It is!"

"Well guess what," I say, whispering. She leans closer toward me like I am about to tell her a secret. "My name is Ruthia! Our names are so alike!" She squeals! Lord, how I love little kids. They're just so animated.

"Yeah!" she exclaims and offers me her hand. I shake it, but instead of letting go, she pulls me somewhere. I hurry into a standing position as she drags me into a room; I glance up right before we pass through the doorway and see a sign saying New Home

Daycare.

I'd actually applied there for my practicum but hadn't heard from them. The smell of graham crackers and apple juice assaults my senses, and there are little kids everywhere. From the ages of 2-4, all different sizes and in different stages of development and each accompanied by a mother. I am wondering why until I see a big sign saying: Mommy and Me written in crayon by the kids. It is just too adorable.

I glance at little Cynthia. "Where's your mommy, sweetheart?"

Her whole face drops. "Mommy didn't come. I told her about today, but she just left me here." My heart breaks for her. There's nothing worse than feeling like you're not cared for. I know how that feels. And then her head snaps up, and she smiles.

"I have an idea!" Her excitement almost masks the nerves in her voice - almost.

"What is it, honey?"

"Will you be my mommy today?" she fiddles with the ball in her hands and bites her lip. My heart warms at her question, and I give her a big smile.

"I would love to be your mommy today, Cynthia!" Her smile is nearly blinding, her eyes sparkle, and she squeals while jumping up and down. I giggle and crouch down to give her a big hug, and she squeezes me back. While in this position, I quickly scan the room to see if I can find who's in charge. Bingo, a Black woman with short navy hair is walking around without a child attached to her. She looks to be in her mid-thirties, but it's hard to tell with Black women. We age so slowly.

"We are going to have so much fun!"

"We definitely will! I just need to talk to someone first and then I'll be right back." I assure her, and she smiles back at me.

"Okay."

I make haste at approaching the woman and tap her on the shoulder to get her attention.

"Hi, do you work here or are you another mom?" I ask, checking to see if my guess is correct.

She nods. "Yes, my name is Michelle. I recently took over ownership of this daycare."

"Congratulations! My name is Ruthia. Little Cynthia over there," I gesture toward Cynthia, who is patiently waiting with the ball in her hand, "requested that I act as her substitute mother for the day. I just wanted to check in with you if that's okay. I'm an ECE student at Sheridan and have a copy of my vulnerable sector check on my phone if you need it."

"Thank you for checking in with me. I appreciate that, and I would love the help today. You'd think it'd be more restful with the moms here instead of more stressful." She shakes her head and then smiles at me. "Go enjoy your time with Cynthia, and let me know if you need anything."

"Great, thanks!" I smile back at her and then head over to where I left Cynthia.

"Alrighty, we're all set. What do you want to do?" I ask her. She holds up the ball with a smile, and I smile back.

A quiet corner, free from many children, provides a space for us to toss the ball. I give her nice slow ones she can catch, and she imitates me. When she tires of catch, we decide to do some coloring together.

I take a moment to observe everything happening around me.

There were kids everywhere, playing and laughing. This one little girl is crying, and her mother holds her, rubbing her back until she relaxes. I smile at that. My mom used to do the same to me.

I close my eyes and hear a voice saying, "Ruthia, why aren't you listening to me?" I know this voice; it stirs up something in my soul; it's God.

I whisper my reply and since the room is so loud and busy, no one notices me talking to what would appear to be myself. *I haven't heard your voice today until now.*

"Ruthia Walkins, I've been speaking to you all day. You've just had selective hearing." I blush.

"What do you mean, Lord?" And then I have a flashback of earlier with little Cynthia. "I love you, Mommy Ruthia!"

"After that, how can you say that you haven't heard me?" He says, and shame saturates me.

"Lord, I do not want to be a mother right now, and I don't want the reminder of Shane in my child for the rest of my life," I reply, almost ready to cry.

"For my thoughts are not your thoughts, neither are your ways my ways, saith the Lord. For as the heavens are higher than the earth, so are my ways higher than your ways, and my thoughts than your thoughts." He replies, and I instantly recognize the scripture; Isaiah 55: 8-9. "Do you trust my word, Ruthia? Do you trust me? That I know the best for you and right now, this is what I want you to do? Will you have faith that I will help you through this? Your child, Shane, and your future?"

"Yes, yes, and yes, Lord," I reply. "I'm sorry for being so willing to reject Your word and Your will, and I thank You for little Cynthia and how You used her to bring me back to my senses. Thank you so much for not giving up on me."

"You're my daughter. I will never leave you nor forsake you. I will never stop loving you or pursuing you. I love you."

My heart warms and I smile, "I love you too, Lord. Amen."

From that moment with the Lord, that smile wouldn't leave my face for the rest of the day. I watch Cynthia play tag for a little while and join the game myself when Brad tags me. I was chasing the kids—slowly, of course—when Michelle interrupts us to announce lunch. I usher the kids past her into the adjoining room where they were to eat.

Lunch passes by with the mothers—and me—serving the little kids. They love it as we play the part of waitresses, giving them pizza, orange or apple juice, and chocolate chip cookies. Miraculously, everything's tidy, and the children are well-behaved. Each child beams with joy, their faces alight with delight. Especially Cynthia.

She is practically glowing, and I give her all my attention; whether it is playing with her after lunch or watching her play with friends. Whenever she does something she thinks is good, she grasps for my attention, saying, "Did you see that Mommy Ruthia?" and I always reply with validation and encouragement.

At that, she would smile even larger. What surprises–and pleases—me is that soon the other little kids talk to me, play catch with me or colour, or just go to me to hear that they are doing a wonderful job too.

I love every minute. I fall into the role easily and each bright blue, green, or brown eye takes a little piece of my heart as I hear the little voice that accompanies it. The way their tiny hands grip mine as they lead me to a certain part of the room or when those delicate arms wind around me in a hug that seems impossibly snug when considering the hugger's strength.

The other mothers accept me as one of their own, and I get along with them as we play with the kids together. That's incredibly fascinating to learn which brands they reject and endorse for the kids. Foods that different kids love, and books that they read to them at night. It is probably more educational than any parenting class I could've taken in school.

It is when washing my hands during a personal bathroom break I have this thought. And then it hits me. School. Oh crap. How is that going to work?

I feel my heart rate quicken and quickly review all the facts. March 23rd, the day we slept together, remains permanently etched in my memory. Today is April 20th exactly 4 weeks later. Doing the math helps me relax. This is my last semester, anyway. I'd probably be able to graduate without showing that much and then over the summer and fall is when the pregnancy would really impact me.

I think anyway.

In ninth grade, I disregarded the pregnancy information taught in Health Class, and now I regret not paying closer attention. Tears spring to my eyes as

I realize how much I don't know. And before I can make them stop, I hear the door open and see Michelle's reflection in the mirror. Crap.

"Ruthia, is everything alright?" It's her kind voice that gets me, and the tears fall. "Oh dear, please don't cry." She says, wrapping her arms around me. I feel her warmth and am soon comforted, drawing back and drying my face with my shirt sleeve. She holds out a few tissues to me, and I offer a wobbly smile. "Would you mind telling me what you were crying about, dear?"

"I just found out this morning that I'm pregnant, and my boyfriend left me, and my dad is a pastor, and he's going to kill me, and I, I just broke."

She looks at me and then sits on the counter, patting a space beside her. I scoot up in the space she's shown and just stay silent; mortified at what I'd just done. Crying in front of a woman I know nothing about and telling her my biggest secret (not that it would stay secret for long, but still) was completely out of character for me. I wonder if hormones can take the blame for this? I feel my cheeks warm and keep my head down.

"Ruthia. Thank you for telling me this. I was in the same position as you, except I still had a year of high school to go because I was 17." My head snaps up quickly, and I see that although she sounds calm, her hands are gripping the counter tightly. "And unlike you, I couldn't deal with it, and I aborted my baby." Her voice cracks with pain, and she shuts her eyes for a few seconds, almost as if she is trying to stop her tears. I am about to reach for some tissue when she takes a deep breath, opens her eyes, and looks directly into mine. "You don't know how much I admire you for what you are about to undergo. I gave up my child, and that's why I work here. My dedication to these children compensates for my past mistakes." She gives me a grateful smile.

"God worked on my heart and I know that I'm forgiven for what I did. And that He's using that motherly love now in this profession. Having been a Christian for close to 10 years, our Heavenly Father will be by your side throughout this. He can soften hearts, Ruthia, and you just need to trust that He has a plan." Her voice becomes stronger and calmer as she speaks these words. She squeezes my hand, giving me a warm smile. I smile back. That same peace that had eased her was now doing the same with me.

"I want you to know that if there's any way that I can help you, let me know. Children adore you; you'll be a fantastic mother. After your life settles down, apply for a job here."

Gratitude rises within me. "I don't know what to say, but thank you, thank you so very much. My coming here now makes even more sense to me. Your words have helped me more than I can say, and I'm so honoured that you shared your story with me. I will apply for the job." I reach over to hug her. She hugs me back tightly. We pull back, smiling at each other, and then randomly start laughing together.

Joy does that to people.

We hop off the counter, and she gestures to a stall. "I actually needed to use the washroom." She tells me, the laughter still in her voice.

I giggle and then nod. "Alrighty, I'll see you out there, Michelle." I leave that washroom so light that it's like I'm flying.

I am just playing catch with Cynthia again when Michelle clears her throat. The room quiets, and we give her our attention.

"It is now 3 o'clock, and it's time for everyone to go home. I want to thank the children for behaving, all the mothers and our honorary mother, Ruthia, for coming today." We clap and my cheeks warm as I receive several warm smiles around the room from mothers and their kids.

Everyone packs up except for Cynthia and me. We sit on the floor with our legs crossed and roll a ball between us; playing hot potato until we are the last ones in the room. "Mommy is sometimes late to pick me up," Cynthia bows her head. "Sometimes, I think she forgets me." My heart breaks at those words.

"Cynthia, look at me, please." She looks at me, and I see the tears forming in her eyes. "Listen to me, your mommy loves you very much, and she will never forget you. She loves you." She nods but looks skeptical. "And I love you, and I'll be there for you whenever you need me, okay?" and then comes her big smile.

She nods and then surprises me by jumping up and throwing her arms around my neck; giving me an exuberant hug. I laugh in surprise and hug her back tightly. When her arms loosen, I release her and then tickle her. Her laugh is loud as she tries to tickle me back, to no avail.

"Cynthia?" At once, both our heads turn toward the voice saying her name. And then Cynthia squeals in glee. "Mommy!" she yells as she runs toward a woman standing in the doorway and wraps her arms around her legs. I laugh and see that Cynthia has most of her looks from her mom.

She has straight dark hair pulled into a bun on the top of her head, a complexion darker than Cynthia's, but the same eyes. Laughing at Cynthia's animation, she leans down and pulls her into a tight hug. "It's great to see you too, Cynthia!"

I get up from my position on the floor and go over to the two of them. "Your daughter was a delight today. You're very lucky to have her." I hope she hears the sincerity in my voice.

"Thank you, and you are?" I stiffen at the suspicion lacing her tone.

"That's Mommy Ruthia! She was my mommy today!" Cynthia answers before I even have the chance, and I feel my cheeks warming again.

"I guess little Thia here just answered that question, but my name is Ruthia Walkins." I offer her my hand.

She shakes it, her grip firm. "My name is Rarity. Thank you for standing in for me today. Do you have any plans right now?"

"None actually. I was just going to take the bus home."

"Anyone capable of making my daughter happy shouldn't need to do all of that. Would you like to come over to get something to eat, and we'll take you home afterwards?" I am about to politely decline her invitation when I glance at Cynthia and see how excited she is.

"Thank you for the invitation. That sounds

wonderful," I reply, and Cynthia jumps with joy. Rarity and I laugh in unison, and I excuse myself so that I can say bye to Michelle.

"Thank you for everything today."

"No, honey, thank you! How about we exchange information so we can keep in touch?" We add our numbers to each other's phones and exchange Instagram handles.

I follow Rarity and Cynthia through the side entrance outside and am surprised to see a car waiting for us. I mean, I expected Rarity to have a car outside, but I didn't realize that she had her own driver and everything. The car is sleek and black and large, similar to a mini limo. I have no clue what car it is, but Shane would know.

Shane.

I feel a pain in my stomach; not cramps or hunger, nor needing to poo or upchuck. It is like my heart clenched, and I was literally feeling the pain. And then Cynthia takes my hand and pulls me into the car. Her smile eases the pain, and I find myself able to smile back. Her mom had gone in first and then Cynthia, putting her in between both of us.

The driver expertly maneuvers through the city's streets. Cynthia tells Rarity about her day and then she falls asleep.

"So, it's safe to say that she had fun today, eh?" Rarity says with a hint of laughter in her voice, and I chuckle.

"I can't believe she just passed out like that, one-minute animation, the next: gone."

Rarity laughs, "I still get surprised sometimes at how she can easily transition to and from sleep. She ends up napping around now until 6. I love that she's resting, but it messes up her sleep pattern because she ends up staying up late and then cannot wake up in the morning."

"Sounds kind of like me when I was younger. I wouldn't ever be able to wake up. My mother needed drastic measures—light, open curtains, and removed sheets—to wake me."

"Same with me! I never used to be a morning person. Then I began early morning jogs while the world slept. It was …"

"Breathtaking." I finish for her, and Rarity nods in agreement. "I started doing the same thing. The world's innocence is most clear at dawn."

"That's exactly how I feel. It's just so much easier to feel like the world isn't a completely horrible place when the air is crisp. there's a slight breeze, and you're just moving."

I am about to reply when we come to a stop.

"Oh, we're here! Thank you, Brian." Rarity says to the driver with the utmost kindness and then gathers the sleeping Cynthia into her arms. Her head drops on Rarity's shoulder, and her tiny hands grasp at the loose tendrils of Rarity's hair. My heart melts at the adorable scene. I open the door for Rarity to go through and then follow her, thanking Brian for the ride.

We are at a classy apartment building near Downtown Brampton, probably one of the newer condos recently constructed. There is actually a doorman who tips his hat to us as we walk in. I give him a warm smile and follow Rarity into an elevator. We stop at the second to last floor, the 9th floor.

Rarity gives me Cynthia and then takes her keys out of her purse, opening the door directly across from the elevator. The door opens to the most beautiful apartment I've ever seen.

It's all earth tones; bronze, different shades of brown and green. Many paintings, each bearing Rarity's corner signature, adorn the walls. Rarity gestures for me to follow her to a room down the hall to the left and opens the door to what looks like Cynthia's room.

It was in shades of purple and bronze, with a huge canopy bed and warm fuzzy rugs. I gently place Cynthia in bed, and her mom pulls the cover over her. She kisses her gently on the forehead and brushes away some hair that is falling onto Cynthia's face. It is so obvious that Rarity loves her daughter.

We leave the room on tiptoe, and Rarity leads me back to the front door.

"Now, I can welcome you to our home. This is our penthouse that takes up a third of this floor. You know already that Cynthia's room is down that hall, where you can also find the other two bedrooms, one being the master for me and ... well, just me. Across the hall is the guest bedroom. Every bedroom includes a private bathroom. The adjacent hall houses the kitchen, a bathroom, an office, and a developing library. In front of us, there's the living room, dining room, and a door to the balcony."

I marvel at the size and beauty of where they live. "You have a stunning home, Rarity."

"Thank you. Would you like some tea and a snack? We can also order in."

"Tea sounds fabulous." I follow her through the

other hall into a kitchen filled with stainless steel appliances, marble counters, deep brown cupboards with glass doors and a breakfast bar with three comfy-looking stools.

I sit on one of them as Rarity prepares tea for both of us. "Peppermint?" she asks.

I nod. "That's my favourite,"

"Same here."

I watch her move with ease around the kitchen and soon enough, we have two mugs of tea. "Care to talk in the living room?"

I nod, and we walk down the hall again, being careful not to spill our tea as we settle on a comfy three-seater couch. We sit on the ends with our feet up between us in the middle seat.

I sip my tea. "So, Rarity. I'd like to ask something; however, no worries if you prefer not to answer."

"Ask away."

I plow ahead. "When you were telling me about your master bedroom, you mentioned it was for you, and it sounded like you were going to mention somebody else, but then thought better of it. What's the story behind that?" My words are tentative, as I sense that this may be a sensitive topic.

She takes a few sips of her tea, and the seconds pass by slowly. I almost think that she will not answer. But then she takes a deep breath. "I meant my husband, Cynthia's father, Jacob." My heart breaks as she lets me into her love story turned into tragedy, culminating in him having an affair.

That's when Rarity's tears come. I put down my tea and then go over to her side of the couch, wrapping an arm around her. She rests her head on my shoulder, and I rub her back as she shakes. "The reason I couldn't be with Cynthia today was that I was meeting with our divorce lawyers, dividing up the assets. I get to keep almost everything. He told me point blank that all this would be mine as long as he didn't have to have Cynthia. He wanted to start a new life with his concubine and didn't want Cynthia reminding him of me."

I can't hold back my gasp. How could anyone do that? How could someone not want Cynthia? She is the most adorable little girl I've seen in a long time.

"I just can't believe that the guy I fell in love with could be capable of being such a jackass. I don't think I've ever felt this broken before." Her tears have stopped, but I continued to hug her, just in case. She lifts her head and gives me a grateful smile.

"Goodness me, I'm sorry that I just broke down like that. I usually am not just like this with people I've just met," Rarity says and blushes.

"Don't worry about it. The guy you love breaking your heart can do that to a person." She chuckles as I let go of her and go back to my end of the couch. "You act as if you're speaking from experience, my dear." She says, and I sigh.

"I am. Today, I experienced heartbreak."

"Honey, what happened?"

"So, I had a boyfriend named Shane. We're now over since I told him I'm pregnant. I've accepted it, and I'm going to be the best mama I can be, but my heart still hurts from Shane. I love him, Rarity. Not even past tense; I still love him." My eyes fill with tears again. "And the thing is, now I'm a stereotype;

girl meets boy, they have sex, girl gets pregnant, boy leaves girl."

"So am I actually. A woman marries a businessman, he goes on business trips, he has an affair, and the businessman leaves the woman. We should make a Stereotypes 'R' US Club." Rarity says dryly, and I explode in laughter, and then she does too. And then we're both just laughing, not only at her joke, but I truly believe to release all the tension. When we finally calm down, we're smiling easily.

"So, what are you planning on doing now?" she asks me.

"Well, when I leave here, I have to go tell my parents about the baby," I say flatly. This was not something I was looking forward to. "My dad is going to murder me. A regular dad would be angry, but my dad is a pastor. My life is over."

"I swear, isn't it a commandment to not kill anyone?" Rarity jokes, and I laugh.

"It is, but it is also one to honour your parents, which I didn't do; so I think the commandments are kind of out the window now," I answer, and we laugh together.

"The only advice I can give to you is to meet up with a girlfriend before going home. Get some dinner with your best friend and get in even more comfort beforehand." I hadn't considered that.

"I like that; I'll text Gaelle now and ask her to meet up with me at our favourite Chinese place. I'm craving Chinese, anyway." I say with a laugh.

"Oh, the joy of cravings. I think I ate a whole watermelon by myself when I was pregnant with Cynthia. Well, let me know what time you want to meet her, and I'll drop you off, okay?"

"Thank you, Rarity." "You're welcome. I know we've just met, but I want to help you in any way I can. From the moment I met you, I could tell that you had a trustworthy and compassionate aura around you."

I don't believe in auras, but I appreciate the kindness meant in her words.

She grabs our mugs, now full of lukewarm tea, and goes to the kitchen to wash them while I workout the details with Gaelle. We text back and forth and once she agrees, Rarity has Brian take me to the restaurant while Cynthia continues to nap.

Gaelle, being the most incredible best friend, already orders for us and as we wait, I fill her in on my upcoming baby. During our dinner, I get a call from Shane, but I just let it ring. Gaelle thinks I should just block him, but I can't bring myself to do that.

When she drops me off at home, I feel better than I had before. But, as I put my key in the front door, dread sweeps over me, and my chest gets tighter; it's time   to   tell   my   parents.

Chapter 4

"Ruthia! Is that you?" I hear my dad call as I walk in through the door.

"No Dad, it's a robber," He laughs at my sarcastic response.

"Did you already get something to eat?"

"Yeah, I had Chinese with Gaelle. I'll just go up into my room now."

"Okay sweetheart!"

That word plagues me as I walk up the stairs and enter my room. I sit on my bed and put my head in between my legs, trying to calm my heart rate.

Sweetheart.

That's what he called me.

Was my confession going to ruin the sweet image I had carefully crafted in his eyes? Just the thought of telling him was freaking me out, without even picturing his face, his tone of voice, how so furious he'd be...

"Oh Lord, help me, please! I need your strength because there's no way that I can tell my parents on my own." My mom interrupts my whispered prayer by entering my room.

"Hey, honey, how was your day? Was school alright?" She sits beside me on the bed, giving me a side hug.

She has done this too many times to count. A lot of my best memories are of us lounging on my bed and talking about life.

About God.

And purity.

And waiting for the man that God has for me.

Those same memories that would warm and comfort my heart are now needles, pricking it repeatedly; causing it to feel pain that is growing more and more intense as it continues.

I just need to get it over with. I could do this. I had to do this. This problem isn't easily fixable.

"My day was ... well, to begin right off. I didn't go to my classes today."

"You skipped school? That is not like the daughter I raised. Who are you, what planet are you from, and where have you put my daughter?" Though she tries to appear stern, a playful demeanor peeks through. I love her and I am about to disappoint her so much.

"Well, if you think that's out of character, get ready for this. I have a lot of things to share with you that you will not believe."

"Try me." I think she still thinks that I am joking, but I am going to go through with this.

"I've been dating this guy for over a year now behind you and Daddy's back. He's really great, Mommy, and we've kept God at the center of our relationship. We've been doing devotionals together. We normally hang out with our group of friends." I gauge her reaction, and she looks surprised, but not mad.

"But that weekend when the church surprised you and Dad with that trip, we were just hanging out in the living room, and things got serious, and we... ended up sleeping together." I take a deep breath, staring down at my bed, the pattern of my covers blurring before me.

"I know you're disappointed in me and that I've failed you. I'm your almost perfect little girl. I'm supposed to be your classy, chaste Ruthia and instead, I've been living a lie. And now, I'm... I'm pregnant." The first teardrops fall. "I've shamed all those talks we'd had, devaluing them in my actions. I know–", my voice breaks, "- you must hate this person sitting beside you. This alien who has so royally messed up. I'm so sorry, Mommy. I'm so sorry."

The pain in my heart grows to where I can barely breathe, and then I feel nothing. Like, my heart has endured so much that it isn't able to feel anymore. It has gone numb. Frozen. And I feel it falling so fast into a dark abyss of nothingness, sure that it will either break or never resurface again.

And then I feel an arm go around me. My heart stops falling.

Her hand rubs my back. My heart thaws.

"Oh Bella, please don't cry." She whispers. "You are my daughter. Not an alien, my daughter. How could I ever hate you? This is nothing compared to my love for you."

Warmth.

Honesty.

Compassion.

She still claims me.

She still wants me.

She still loves me.

Each truth being whispered to me by my mother takes out the needles of lies in my heart. The numbness fades away. The pain is disappearing. The strangling of my heart has ceased.

I can finally breathe.

Still, there is doubt in my mind. Is she serious? Does she really still love me?

I open my eyes to be staring into the ones that I inherited.

They are bloodshot. She has been crying with me.

They are scanning my face, checking to see how I am.

They are full of love, and I have no more doubt.

"Thank you, Mommy." I throw my arms around her. "Thank you."

She smiles. "So, when exactly am I going to be a grandmother?"

I don't know who laughs first, but we are both rolling on the bed laughing almost immediately. The tension leaves the room. The laughter is cleansing. We both sit up breathless and smiling.

"That's how I love to see my Ruthia, with a smile on her face." She says and somehow my smile grows larger. Then she gets off the bed and offers me her hand. "Time to tell your father."

The smile leaves my face. "He's going to kill me, Mom."

"Nah, I don't think so. You overestimate your father. Now c'mon." I take her hand and allow her to pull me off the bed. She pulls me into another hug and says, "It's all going to be okay."

And like always when my mother says that, I believe her.

We go downstairs to find my dad leaning back in his desk chair with a satisfied smile on his face.

"Write something good, Daddy?" Can he hear the

nerves in my voice?

"Yes, sweetheart. I know it will definitely touch some hearts this Sunday. My fingers couldn't type what the Holy Spirit was telling me fast enough." He jokes, his eyes shining. He is full of joy at this moment.

I gulp as I realize I am about to ruin that. "Daddy, I have something important to tell you."

"Go ahead, sweetheart. I'm all ears." He says, still smiling.

"It's not good, Daddy." He frowns for an instant and then laughs.

"Well, it's not like you're pregnant or something Thia, go ahead."

Mom looks at a picture on the wall. I look at the floor. From us, you can hear one unified sound: silence.

His laugh is the only thing audible in the room. "Come now Thia, don't play around with your old man like this. What was it you needed to tell me?"

Silence.

I glance at him to see his eyes grow wide as he realizes why I have yet to refute his comment.

"You're not… you can't be pregnant. You haven't even had sex!" His voice is incredulous.

Silence. I look at the floor again. Could it swallow me up? Any minute now would be nice.

"You're not even seeing anyone, for goodness' sake!" his voice has a tinge of anger to it now.

Silence. I look at the stairs. How quickly can I get up there and jump out of my window?

"Dammit, Ruthia! What is going on? Look at me!" His voice is all anger now. I take a deep breath and look at him, look at his eyes. He's barely holding it together. The last string reigning him in is hope that I am just joking with him.

And snip, snip goes the scissors.

"I'm pregnant." I breathe out the words, hoping that the volume will weaken their impact.

No dice.

I watch my dad transform before my very eyes. The light, that thin ray of hope, leaves him. His whole body clenches, and his hands tighten into fists. He takes a step toward me, and I flinch.

"How." It doesn't even sound like a question, though I know it is.

"I've had a secret boyfriend for the past 14 months."

He repeats louder this time, "How."

"The night you and mom went to Niagara Falls, we were hanging out and then one thing led to another." I cringe at the use of cliché.

"How." He's speaking in his normal voice now.

"I don't know! The pill I'm on didn't work?"

"HOW COULD YOU HAVE BEEN SO STUPID? HOW COULD YOU BE MY DAUGHTER? HOW?" He yells, throwing his desk chair against the wall.

I'm shaking now. My mother moves toward me and wraps her arms around me, trying to still my tremors.

"Harry, calm down." My mother intervenes. "You are scaring her."

"Good! Let fear grip her! Clearly, fear hadn't gripped her enough. She did not have the fear of God in her, as I had thought. This person who you are holding is a big woman who has nothing to be afraid of." He paces back and forth over the course of the tirade. Then he halts in front of me.

"What could have possessed you to … I can't even say it." His disgust is apparent.

"He said he loved me."

"LOVE?" He laughs in my face. "Every guy knows I love you is the password to get into a girl's pants. I cannot believe that you fell for that!"

"He wasn't like that. That's not what he was after."

"Oh yeah? And where is he now? Does he know? Does he care?" Each question is like a knife in the back, and I can't answer. "That's what I thought. You screwed up your life for a guy who couldn't even get a proper condom." His laugh is bitter. "Who is the father?"

"It doesn't matter because he's no longer a part of my life anymore."

"I demand to know who the father is." His voice is scary quiet. Despite the fear I should feel, I'm thinking of Shane.

I don't know who my father is right now.

I don't trust my father right now.

I will not tell him about Shane.

I still love him.

Yes, he made it clear how he felt earlier. Yes, he wants nothing to do with me.

Yes, he broke my heart.

But, I still love him, and I will protect him in this way.

"I refuse to tell you who he is."

"THIS WAS NOT AN OFFER. WHO IS HE?"

My ears feel like they are about to explode, but I stand my ground.

"I. Will. Not. Tell. You." I force out the words, my hands balling up into fists.

His arm moves so fast that it's a blur. I feel myself land on the floor. My arm moves to the right side of my face. Where he'd hit me.

My father has never laid a hand on me in my life.

I look up at him in horror and then hear a scream. "Harry, stop it! Are you out of your mind? She is WITH CHILD." My mother is wringing her hands and shaking. I have never seen her like this before.

"That is the problem, Emiline! And your way of talking with her over the years didn't work. So maybe let me handle this." My mother flinches.

If looks could harm, my father would be on a gurney right now.

I would be six feet under.

My mother rushes up the stairs and then my dad turns back to me.

"Then. I. Will. Kick. You. Out."

I look into his eyes to see if there's a small part of him that isn't serious. There is none.

"Then I guess you're kicking me out."

His eyes widen, he wasn't expecting that. He goes to the front door and opens it while I step into the sneakers I'd left at the front earlier. I'm surprised to see a car outside and then I hear her voice.

"Bella!" I turn around to see my mom coming toward me.

"Here's your purse, a duffle bag with the essentials, and your backpack for school." She says, giving these things to me and then enveloping me in a big hug. "I love you." She whispers. I feel her tears on my neck.

"I love you too," We pull away and then I face my father.

My father, whose face used to light up when I walked into the room, who read me bedtime stories when I was younger, who taught me how to burp and spit, who asked me to read over his sermons and give him my opinion.

I can't even recognize him. My anger disappears, and only sadness remains.

"Goodbye Daddy."

"Don't call me that. You are deceitful. Stupid. Selfish. Loose. Trashy. Wanton. Disobedient. Disrespectful. Ungrateful. And ugly, deformed by your impurity. I don't know who the hell you are, but you are not my daughter."

Tears spring to my eyes, and I run—right out of the place that used to be my home.

I try to wipe away my tears as I get into the cab. I have to hold it together for at least a little while longer.

And I do.

I tell the driver to just drive away while I take out my phone and open the note where I had typed out Rarity's address. I give him the address and the drive seems like it takes forever and, also, no time at all. It seems like I have no sense of time anymore. When we arrive at the now familiar building, I breathe easier. I pay the driver and thank him for the ride in a daze, hoisting my duffle bag over one shoulder and my backpack on the other, my purse resting on the crook of my elbow.

Just a little longer. I can make it.

The doorman recognizes me and nods me in. I try to give him a smile as I walk into the building, though I doubt it looks like a real one. The elevator comes almost immediately, to my relief. I get off at the 9th floor and knock on Rarity's door. I check my phone. It's just past 8:30.

How could so much happen in one day? I feel like I've aged a million years in the past 16 hours.

The good thing about the time is that Rarity is still awake and comes to the door within a minute of my knocking. She opens the door with a smile that falls as soon as she sees me.

I must look like a mess.

She opens up her arms, and I'm undone. The bags drop from my arms and I'm sobbing into her shoulder. "It's okay." She murmurs to me. "It's all going to be okay."

"We're going to get you all set up in the guest room. Okay?" I try to look appreciative, but I can barely lift the corners of my mouth into a smile. She grabs my bags with no problem and leads me down the hall where we had put Cynthia to sleep. She opens the door to the room directly across from it and gestures for me to go in.

Even in my disoriented state, I can see and admire the beauty of the room. It's beautiful, adorned in different shades of blue with gold and bronze accents throughout. Rarity puts down my things on an oak dresser and then sits down on the bed, patting a spot beside her.

Like a robot, I sit down.

"Can you tell me what happened?" Caution laces

her tone.

I shake my head no.

Rarity nods and gives me another hug. Then she gets up and takes off my shoes for me. She puts them in a corner of the room and then comes back to pull back the covers of the bed. After doing so, she takes one of my hands and tugs a bit, gesturing to where she'd just pulled back the covers. I obediently get up and go into the spot that she'd prepared. She tucks me in and heads to the door, about to shut off the light when we both hear, "Mommy Ruthia? Is that you?"

"Yes, honey, it's her. But Ruthia's not feeling well right now. She's going to go to sleep. You can talk to her tomorrow," Rarity says in a quiet voice.

Cynthia ignores her and runs up to where I'm lying in the bed. "Mommy Ruthia, you look like you've been crying."

I muster all the emotion and energy I have left to give her a genuine smile. "I'm going to be alright, sweetheart, don't worry. I just need some sleep." She nods, almost reassured, and then her whole face lights up.

"I have an idea! Wait one second!" She runs out of the room and she's back within seconds, breathless. "Here you go!" She thrusts a white teddy bear toward me. "Her name is Terra. She always makes me feel better when I'm sad. She can make you feel better too!" What's left of my heart melts.

"Thank you, sweetheart. She's already making me feel better." I sit up slightly, opening my arms to give her a hug. She goes right into them and hugs me tight. Then Cynthia pushes me down and tucks me back into bed with Terra in my arms.

"Goodnight, Mommy Ruthia." She kisses me on the forehead.

I smile and look at Rarity. She's in tears, smiling proudly at her daughter. "Now come on, honey. Let's let Ruthia sleep and get you ready for bed." She holds out her hand. Cynthia runs toward her mother, grabs Rarity's hand tightly, and they leave the room, Rarity shutting off the light as they do so.

With them gone, it's like light has left the room. Left alone, all I can hear are my father's *last words to me.*

Deceitful.

Stupid.

Selfish.

Loose.

Trashy.

Wanton.

Disobedient.

Disrespectful.

Ungrateful.

You are not my daughter.

You are not my daughter.

You are not my daughter.

I cry myself to sleep.

Chapter 5

I am on campus, walking toward one of the student lounges. My reflection from the glass wall beside me morphs into my dad, startling me. "You are not my daughter."

I become stone and look around me, but no one else has seen it.

To take my mind off of what happened today, I head to the library finding some books that look up to distract me. As I'm checking them out, I see my reflection in a nearby computer screen become him once again, saying: "You are not my daughter".

I run, trying to escape his expression. His eyes are hard and unfeeling, his features distorted in anger and disgust, and his voice saying those words. I can hear them on repeat in my ears.

As a last resort, I go to the place that has always comforted me. I climb the steps to see that my dad is there.

No reflection, him in the flesh.

He stands in front of the church, arms crossed, and peers down at me like I am tainting the church by being at its entrance.

"What are you doing here?" He takes a step

toward me. I take a step back. "This is not a place for you. You do not deserve to be here. You devalue this area with your presence." The vehemence in his voice causes me to take another step back, but I trip over and fall on the concrete. Pain creeps up my back and I can't move. He laughs and comes beside my strewn-out body.

"You are deceitful. Stupid. Selfish. Loose. Trashy. Wanton. Disobedient. Disrespectful. Ungrateful. And ugly, deformed by your impurity." With every sentence, he kicks my side. Repeatedly. I cry at the physical and emotional pain. I just barely get enough energy to speak three words.

"Daddy, please stop." They come out as a teary whisper, but I know he hears me. He squats down so that he can look into my eyes.

"You are not my daughter."

I force myself awake.

'It was only a nightmare.' I try to calm my breathing.But I am lying to myself.

My life is the nightmare. The dream had been more of an altered memory than a work of fiction.

His face had looked the same in real life as it had in the dream — thanks to my photographic memory.

His voice dripping in disdain had been an exact replication of what I'd heard before.

And those words.

He had really said them, and he had meant it.

I shiver, though I'm wrapped in a comforter, and then feel the bile rise in my throat.

I get out of bed as quickly as possible and then scan the room for the door that leads to the washroom.

There. Right across from me. Is it a closet or my

refuge? I go to it and open the door to, thank God, the washroom. I barely have time to rejoice over my correct guess before I lean over the toilet retching up Chinese food.

The cold from the tiled floor seeps through my pants, and I shiver uncontrollably, unable to stop myself from falling onto the floor.

I am disgusted by myself.

No wonder Shane didn't want to stick around.

No wonder my dad has disowned me as his daughter.

And God, He probably doesn't want me either.

I curl into a ball and cry. My breaths become more and more shallow, my chest becoming more and more tight. Another anxiety attack.

I don't know how much time passes before I hear the buzzing sound.

Great, now I'm hallucinating.

I try to calm myself down and regulate my breathing to stop my brain's journey to insanity. But I still hear the buzzing, even clearer than before.

It's my phone.

I sit up and peek into the bedroom, straining my eyes to see that the dresser that Rarity put my things on is just a few feet away from the washroom. It takes all the energy I have to get myself up and standing, then head over to the dresser. I find my purse and dig through it until my fingers have wrapped around my phone.

I slide my thumbs across the screen to answer the call. I hold it up to my ear and open my mouth to say something, but nothing comes out.

There is a heartbeat of silence on the line and

then, "Ruthia?"

It's Gaelle.

It feels like I have heard none other voice but my father's for so long.

Her voice is the exact opposite of his, tender and full of … love.

Hearing that in her voice, I break down again and all I can do is lean on my bags and cry.

"Shhh. Thia. It's okay. Sis, it's okay. It's all going to be okay, *ma chère*. I promise." She keeps repeating those words over and over again as I cry. Her words are like a warm hug comforting me.

"Dear Heavenly Father, thank You. Thank You for waking me up from my nap and telling me to call my sister Ruthia. Father, it kills my heart to hear my sister in such pain. Lord–" her voice cracks and then I realize that she's crying as well. "Lord. Please, give her Your peace right now." The ball of stress in my stomach eases, and I can breathe. "Lord, please wipe away her tears." My tears flow slower and slower. "Lord, please wrap Your arms of love around Your daughter." I feel myself encased in warmth and love. "Lord, let her know she is so loved. Father, please remind her soul that You are her joy, You are her strength, and You are her Father."

At these words, I straighten up. He is my Father. Father. Father. My mind brings the last image of my dad back to mind, and my knees buckle. I feel like I am being held down, and I can't get up. Gaelle's voice continues, getting stronger. "Jesus. Jesus. Jesus. In the name of Jesus, I bind and cast out all the spirits that are terrorizing my sister right now. Lord, I cast out shame. I cast out guilt. I cast out self-hate." I feel myself getting lighter. I literally feel things coming off me, and I mouth words I do not understand, but know are from the Holy Spirit within me. Gaelle continues, "I cast out everything that is not of You, right now. For You defeated it all on the cross. My sister has freedom from these things as a slave to You, to righteousness. She is no longer bound by them. And I declare her freedom right now. Satan, you will *not* have her life. I rebuke you and your schemes in the name of Jesus. You are defeated and have no place here. Leave my sister. *Now.*" Her voice is angrier than I'd ever heard her, and it startles me so much that I open my eyes.

It's impossible. To my utter surprise, I see darkness rising out of the room. Like a layer of muck being removed from the air. It's sinister, but I'm not scared. I feel myself wrapped in the love of my Father.

And I know, *I know*, that He has already conquered this darkness.

"Ruthia, declare who you are right now in Christ. Speak truth to the lies that have been shredding away at your soul," Gaelle says in the most serious voice I've heard from her.

"I am free. I am fearfully and wonderfully made." I almost feel as if Gaelle is right in front of me, nodding at me encouragingly, like when we study together at the library. This makes me smile. "I am created with purpose and so is this baby. My God, my Father, my King; He is bigger than anything and everything I have and will ever face." I see the darkness become smaller.

"Keep going."

"I am more than a conqueror in Christ Jesus." It is decreasing in size now.

"That's it, Thia."

"I am the daughter of the Most High God." An enormous chunk of the darkness disappears.

"Declare it sister."

"I. Am. Loved." There goes another huge part of it.

"Hallelujah. Hallelujah."

"And no matter who rejects, leaves, or judges me. My God, my Saviour, and my Advocate will *never* leave me or forsake me. And because of that, I will always have more than enough." I am filled with strength and passion as I declare these words.

And the darkness is gone.

The room is still dark. However, this darkness is normal. It's natural. The *supernatural* darkness that was here is now gone.

I go down on my knees, close my eyes and bow my head.

"Thank You, Jesus. Thank You, Father. Thank You for Your truth that has set me free, Your love that has warmed me from the inside out, and Your light that has banished the darkness. And thank You, Lord, for my sister. You've truly blessed me by placing this prayer warrior and spiritual soldier into my life. In Your name, Amen."

"Amen." Gaelle also says into the phone. I get up from my position on the floor and lean against the dresser. "Thia." She says my name with more emotion than I thought possible. It holds warmth, pride, joy, peace, and love. All at once.

"Elle." Tears prick at my eyes once more.

Somehow, she can tell.

"Oh, no, you don't. Don't you go crying on me again! You've used up your tears limit for the year, Ruthia." I laugh at her teasing.

"I love you, Elle. Only you could make me laugh right now."

"I love you too, Thia. Sisters for forever..."

"...Times infinity and beyond."

There's a comfortable silence and then Gaelle laughs.

"You realize that doesn't make grammatical sense, right?" I replay the words in my head, realizing that she's right. I join in on her laughter.

"We were 6. We put everything at that age to the power of infinity and beyond, or it wasn't legit."

"Gosh, I love us."

"Agreed." I flop onto the bed in the room, content.

"So, are you going to fill me in on what has happened to you since I saw you last?" Always getting to the point, that girl.

I gave her an overview of my parents' reactions and how I was now staying at Rarity's. She whistles.

"No wonder HS woke me up and had me call you." Her shock becomes sympathy. "I'm so sorry, Thia."

"Not your fault, but thanks, Elle. Seriously, thank you. You didn't have to listen to HS. You could've gone back to sleep, chosen to read a book, or called me in the morning. Thank you, Gaelle."

"Anytime, anything for you, sis."

I smile, "You know you are *so* going to be the godmother, right?"

"Really?"

"Of course. My child is going to need to have such a powerful prayer warrior in their

life."

"I'm honoured, Thia."

"I love you, Elle. Always know."

"I will. Now, try to get back to sleep. It's like 3 in the morning. You need your rest."

"Yes, doctor."

She laughs, "I still have about 6 more years of school left before that happens, but I'm glad you still have your sass." She yawns. "And it seems my body also feels that it needs to rest. I'll talk to you soon. Je t'aime."

"Je t'aime, Elle."

I glance at the time on my phone after hearing the click of Gaelle hanging up. She was pretty on point with the time. It was 3:01 on the dot. Doing the math, I realized I had only told my parents about my pregnancy, give or take seven hours ago.

Seven hours.

Maybe we should find a different way to measure time, because those seven hours felt like seven lifetimes of my soul being tortured, of living death, of hell.

But God.

I don't know if I've ever valued or appreciated His presence so much until now, because I'd never really felt such an absence of it before.

And I don't think that I'd ever taken spiritual warfare that seriously until now, either. I know that when Jesus was doing his ministry, He cast out demons. It's easy to believe in Canada that supernatural warfare and malevolent spirits are things of the past. I'm glad about Gaelle's Haitian heritage. Her family used to practice voodoo, but then her grandmother came to faith and changed the course of her family. Because of that, her family has always been serious about spiritual warfare, and Gaelle has always prayed with such authority. I know that this is where my learning about spiritual warfare begins, and I am now willing to be an eager student.

I feel the need to yawn, and I abruptly cut short my mental monologue.

I'll be an enthusiastic student all right—as soon as I get some sleep.

My eyes close, but I stop myself.

'Come on Ruthia. Get up, find your toothbrush and toothpaste, flush the toilet, brush your teeth and *then* go to bed.'

Sighing, I follow the directions from the voice of reason in my head in a sleep-like state. And then—feeling fresh in body and spirit—I go back underneath the covers, grab Terra, and fall into a peaceful sleep.

Chapter 6

I feel a hand rubbing my back and another pushing back my hair, making me think that it's my mom waking me up. And then all the memories come back like a soft voice, whispering everything that has passed to me.

I know that's the Holy Spirit.

I open my eyes to see Rarity sitting on the bed. She's the one who is waking me up.

"Good morning." Her voice is both cheerful and cautious. The caution in her voice is no doubt because of the mess I was when she opened her door for me.

I smile to let her know that I'm better, much better than before. "Good morning, Rarity." I rub the sleep guck out of my eyes. "What time is it?"

"Five fifteen. I was wondering if you wanted to go on a jog with me this morning?" I'm silent, calculating how much sleep I got in the night to see if I can actually do a proper jog this morning. Rarity mistakes my silence for a rejection. "Or you know, you don't have to. I just figured that we could enjoy seeing the world so pure and innocent at its earliest hours."

My smile widens, remembering that I had uttered

those same words yesterday. "I'd love to, Rarity. Let me just see if I have anything packed that I can jog in."

"Really? Okay, good then! See you in about ten minutes at the front of the apartment." I hear the surprise and happiness in her voice. She must be so nervous, taking in this random girl who looked like death the night before. She gets up, but I touch her arm to stop her.

"Thank you, Rarity, for everything. I want you to know that I'm okay. I've made a total 180 from last night." I can tell that she sees the truth in my words and then she breathes. In doing so, I see a lot of the worry and nerves leave her body. She relaxes and her eyes are now brighter.

"That's good to hear, Ruthia. You had me worried last night, hon. I look forward to hearing about the change that has happened to you."

"I look forward to telling you." I sit up and reach out my arms. We hug, and I thank God once more for sending this woman into my life.

We pull back, smiling, and then she gets up and leaves me to get ready.

I get out of bed and head to the bathroom. Like I do every morning, I brush my teeth while picking out what to wear—multitasking like this saves me a lot of time. Though, this morning, my clothes are in a duffel bag instead of in my closet and drawers. I empty the contents of my duffel bag onto the—my—bed and see that my mom had thought of everything.

She packed me three pairs of jeans, two jogging pants, two sweaters, three cardigans, maybe seven tank tops and V-neck shirts and tons of underwear.

Underneath it all is the toiletries bag I had already gotten into last night—err, this morning. One compartment held my deodorant, lotion, body wash, shampoo, and conditioner. The other holds all my jewelry, combs, and other hair accessories. On the side compartment of the duffel, I find two pairs of flats and a few pairs of colourful socks along with the chargers for my phone and laptop.

Emiline Walkins is a boss at packing.

Since I am already wearing jogging pants, I just change my shirt and grab a sweater. Oh, and apply deodorant. I sniff myself and cringe. A lot of deodorant.

It's a perfect Friday morning. I feel refreshed as I breathe in the crisp morning air, and the slight breeze moves my braids. Rarity and I are jogging at the same pace toward a park that she loves about half an hour away. We both like to listen to music and be in our own world while we jog; so we decided that once we get to the park, we'll slow to a walk and then talk. When Rarity taps me on the shoulder and gestures for me to follow her on the path leading into the park, I'm surprised. It feels like no time has passed at all.

Rarity slows to a walk, and I follow suit, awed by the beauty of our surroundings. There is green everywhere, like the trees have woken up from the winter. I see little flowers of different colours beginning to bloom, like dots of colour on a green canvas. It's beautiful.

"Ruthia, over here." I understand why she whispers. The peace and beauty of this place seem almost sacred. I look up to see that she's far ahead of me and about to make a turn. I didn't even realize that

I'd fallen behind looking at everything around me.

She waits for me to catch up to her and leads me onto a little brick bridge. We lean against the railing, and I glance down. The stream running underneath it is clear and beautiful. I even see the beginning blooms of aquatic plants. "Ruthia, look up." I obey and my breath catches in my throat.

It's the perfect view of dawn.

We watch the sun climb into the sky in silence. There must be a million different shades before me right now. The only sound to be heard is the wind in the trees, rustling the leaves—almost like it's applauding the ascension of the sun. A verse instantly comes to mind.

God is in the midst of her, she will not be moved; God will help her when morning dawns. - Psalm 46:5

I whisper the verse aloud, catching Rarity's attention in doing so.

She turns to face me. "What was that?"

"Oh, just a Bible verse that had popped into my head. 'God is in the midst of her, she will not be moved; God will help her when morning dawns' found in Psalm chapter 46, verse 5."

Rarity repeats the words to herself with a smile. "That is beautiful, Ruthia. Totally beautiful."

I smile back. "Those are David's words, I think, not mine. Always have to cite my sources."

She chuckles. "I remember having to do those works cited pages, gosh that feels like ages ago. I always hated them. They were tedious and time-consuming."

"Preach it, sister!"

Rarity laughs and then a dark shadow seems to

pass over her face. "Speaking of preaching ... and pastors ... Ruthia ... what happened last night?"

I sigh. "A lot."

"Understatement, I'm presuming?" I laugh at her sass and she smiles. "C'mon, let's continue to walk around and you can fill me in."

"So, I got home, greeted my dad and then went straight to my room..." Rarity listens intently as I share what happened last night, not interrupting even once. My voice cracks at my dad's words toward me. She gives me a brief but comforting hug, helping me to compose myself and continue the tale. By the time I reach the end, Rarity is stunned.

"So, you're saying that she prayed with you and from that you went from a mess to this?" Rarity is not buying this.

"Prayer is a powerful thing." She shakes her head in disbelief and then laughs to herself.

"Man, you must have some type of faith, Ruthia."

"Just faith in who deserves it. God always does." I try to choose my words carefully. "What do you believe in, Rarity?"

"Well, I grew up in the church."

"Really?"

"Yeah, but I drew away from it all around when I left for university. Church was a family thing, and when I was away from my family, church just kind of fell away as well. I still believe that there's a Being out there and a spiritual aspect to the world, but I don't align with religion anymore." There is no hesitation in her words.

I nod in understanding but inwardly cringe. What should I do? Tell Rarity that she is wrong right then and there?

'Ruthia, I have called you for such a time as this.'

And there is His voice. I smile as I feel His peace.

'I want my daughter to come back to me.'

I will do whatever You tell me to, Father. Shall I, for lack of a better word, preach to her right now?

'No, daughter. Your life will be your message. Live as my daughter according to the Spirit within you, and she will see Me. Then, she will come home.'

Lord, I promise to do all you have said. It won't be easy, but I know You will help me represent You in humility and without hypocrisy. I trust Your plan.

And then I felt an unbelievable warmth on my face even though Rarity and I hadn't stepped into a patch of sunlight. I know this is Him, like He is smiling at me.

I love You, Father.

'And I love you, My daughter. Go with My peace and remain in My love.'

"Rarity, are you still okay with me staying with you even though we have different beliefs?"

She stops walking and turns to look at me, taking my hands in hers. "Of course I am, Ruthia. Everything I've seen about you thus far has shown wisdom, kindness, and strength. Your faith is clearly a huge part of you exemplifying those qualities, so how could I mind? I look forward to being an older sister for you through all of this, okay? Don't doubt that." Her earnest response brings tears to my eyes.

Lord, I hate being so emotional. I chalk it up to being pregnant.

"Thank you Rare. I always wanted a big sister."

"You're welcome."

We smile at each other once more and then begin the jog back toward her place—back home.

We get there soon enough, and I immediately take a shower, grabbing a pair of jogging pants, a tank top, a cardigan and undergarments to change into.

The struggle to figure out how to work the shower is more than worth it when the water comes out. I feel as if I am not only cleansing the physical grime of yesterday, but the emotional gunk as well.

I walk into the hallway, humming to myself, and nearly run into Cynthia. She is still in PJs and rubbing the sleep out of her eyes. Upon seeing me, though, her face brightens.

"Mommy Ruthia!"

I laugh and squat down to her height, opening up my arms. "Good morning, Thia! Do I get a morning hug?" she nods enthusiastically and runs into them, nearly toppling me over.

"Looks like someone is awake after all!" Rarity approaches us with a towel and clothes over one arm and lotion in one hand. "Are you ready to take a bath now, sweetheart?"

"Yes, Mommy! Do I get to use the green soap?" I love how animated she is over the littlest things. It's a quality that people seem to lose as we age, which is a shame.

"Yes, you do, hon! C'mon, let's go!" Rarity matches Cynthia's excitement and offers her daughter her empty hand. Cynthia takes it without hesitation and skips alongside her mother.

"See you soon, Mommy Ruthia!"

"Alrighty Thia!" I walk to the kitchen and make myself a cup of tea. I feel myself getting a little nauseous and need to calm my stomach. This morning sickness business does not sit well with me.

It is peaceful to just sit at the breakfast bar and sip my tea. The clock on the stove reads 7:15. Normally, at this time, I would just be finishing up my morning routine. Waiting for the text from Shane that would say he's here to pick me up for breakfast.

My heart pangs at the memories of those mornings of going through the drive-thru at Tim Hortons. The way we would listen to a sermon on the radio while he was driving and then discuss what was being talked about. It was a part of our devotional time when he sharpened the woman of God I am, and vice versa.

I miss him so much, but at least I know I won't have to see him until Monday. I have the entire weekend to prepare myself.

Before I can yield to the wallowing, Cynthia bounds into the kitchen, looking adorable in dark jeans and a green sweater that matches her eyes.

If I have a daughter, I will always dress her beautifully. I promise to myself as I help Cynthia onto a stool.

"So, what shall we do for breakfast today, Thia? Cereal? Waffles? Toast?" Rarity asks as she enters the kitchen, looking comfortable in dark jeans and an army green t-shirt.

"Oh! Waffles!" Rarity raises an eyebrow at Cynthia's squeal. "Please," Cynthia adds in a sheepish voice at a lower volume. Rarity smiles approvingly.

"Sounds good, sweetheart." She takes out a package of Eggo waffles from the freezer, popping a couple into the toaster. "I'll make mine after yours are done. How about you, Thia?”

I can hear my stomach rumble at the thought of waffles. “That sounds excellent, Rare. Can I help with anything?”

“Hmm, want to set the breakfast bar?”

And we continue like that. We fall into an easy pattern around the kitchen; almost like a dance. Swirling around each other and laughing as we do so. Cynthia helps me figure out where each thing is, and it is… fun.

I feel like we are already a family; sitting at the breakfast bar, teasing each other about how much syrup we each used, threatening to touch each other with our fingers sticky from the oranges we’d been eating, and just laughing through it all.

And then Rarity notices the time on the stove, “Oh my goodness! Cynthia, you’re going to end up late for daycare if we don’t leave now.”

“I’ll do the dishes, Rarity. Just get there in time.”

“Thanks, Hon. Come on Cynthia, let’s go see Michelle today!”

“Bye, Mommy Ruthia!”

I give Cynthia a wave goodbye in response.

“I’ll be back in about half an hour, Ruthia. Maybe you should start researching things for your situation.”

I nod in understanding. “Will do, Rare! See you soon.” I give her a brief hug before she leaves, closing and locking the door behind her.

The penthouse seems so empty without the two of them here. It’s odd not to hear Cynthia making noise or Rarity’s calm voice as I walk to the kitchen. To fill the silence, I sing one of my favorite reggae church songs as I start the dishes. “You’ve turned my mourning into dancing again. You've lifted my sorrows. I can't stay silent. I must sing, for your joy has come."

Those two sentences are really the complete song, so I sing them over and over again, dancing to the imaginary music of the church band until the dishes are done, and the counters are spotless. Satisfied, I head over to my bedroom and grab my laptop from my purse to do what Rarity suggested.

I make myself comfortable on my bed and google "What to do when you're pregnant". One of the first few links looks promising, babycenter.com, so I click on it and am led to a page full of steps of what to do now that I'm with child. The first thing they say to do is calculate my due date and they even have a calculator for me to use! I type in the date that Shane and I did the deed and then wait for the date to pop up.

Sunday, November 30th.

The date shocks me and suddenly, I'm numb. The date has me frozen; I can hardly think, and it dominates my thoughts.

Sunday, November 30th.

I'm still in the same position when I hear the key in the lock and Rarity's voice ringing through the apartment.

"Ruthia?"

I open my mouth to answer her, to tell her I'm in my room, but it's like my brain is refusing to send the message to my mouth. I hear footsteps and am thankful when I see Rarity appear in the doorway.

She smiles, relieved to see me, and makes herself comfortable next to me on the bed. She tilts the laptop so that she can see what has me so transfixed.

"So, you did what I said. You started researching your pregnancy." I nod. "And look, you found an excellent website. Good job Thia." I crack a smile. She's encouraged by that and continues. "And after you got on this site, what did you do?"

"It said to calculate my due date." Finally, my vocal cords were working. "So, I typed in the day that Shane and I had ... Well, you know. And this popped up." My voice cracks as I cry.

"Sunday, November 30th. What's wrong, you have something against November babies? Because if you do, that date is not permanent - your child could be born later in December." I actually laugh at her weak joke, making her smile. "So, what's wrong?"

"Nothing's wrong. It's more like I was just given an extreme reality check. I mean, yesterday thrust me into the reality of my situation, but, it's like, I just realized that my child is going to have a birthday. They are going to have parties planned around that day, and receive presents, and have birthday cards. I'll have a child to buy birthday cards for, Rarity. That's crazy!" I raise my arms to emphasize my point and then flop onto the bed. "And people are going to mark that day as special because it will be the day that they came into the world. It's as if everything that comes with being a parent hit me as soon as I saw the day that might be my child's birthday." No wonder my brain had taken an impromptu vacation. I had overloaded it with all those thoughts. Letting them out was relaxing, so I let loose my biggest fear. "And now I have to wonder, what if I'll be a terrible mother, Rarity?! What if -"

"Okay, I'm going to cut you off there. You will

not be a terrible mother."

"But I know nothing about being one, Rarity. Nothing, zilch, nada."

"You have a natural gift with children. Not to mention, you have months to prepare as well, and you have mothers who will help you every step of the way. You do not need to worry about that, okay? Actually, I think I'm going to need a promise from you that you won't ever think/voice those thoughts again. They are nonsense. Promise?"

I smile at her kind words and the no-nonsense way that she delivered them. "Promise."

"That's what I like to hear! Just so you know, I took the day off work so that we can spend some time together. Let's start by looking through everything together, alright?"

"Alright," and off we go.

For the next hour, we look through everything that I'll need to do and everything that I'll need. I wonder, why don't they just teach things in health class? Legit, all the work that accompanies being pregnant, would promote abstinence! After a while, Rarity and I start a to-do list for everything that we'd need for me. The very first thing is setting an appointment for me with her obstetrician/gynecologist, Dr. Sandra Parks. "She's excellent. She helped keep me sane through my pregnancy, and I didn't have a male looking at my lady parts."

"I trust your judgement." My nerves are mounting again, and my leg shakes with all my tense energy. This does not go unnoticed by Rarity.

"Hey, talk to me. What's happening right now?"

"Just some anxiety in my body at realizing all the things that I need to do. I'm so nervous. I am in uncharted water here."

"But you're with someone who has already gone before you, well, gone through this before you, I guess. In me. You will not be alone at any point."

My soul settles at her reassurance. She is right, but not just regarding herself. God has already gone before me. God holds my future and is trustworthy. I will never be alone because I have Him.

"I remember my first ultrasound - it was so surreal. The ultrasound technician and I were both in masks, the ultrasound gel was cool on my skin. I always thought they performed it on the stomach, but because the pregnancy was so early, it was actually much closer to the pelvis. And then the tech let me hear the heartbeat." She pauses, her voice getting emotional.

Clearing her throat, she continues, "I was in awe. That was the moment that it really set in. There was a human growing in my body, and I would already do everything to take care of them. No matter what."

"That's beautiful, Rare."

"Pregnancy is beautiful. It's hard. I will not sugarcoat things for you. But it is so good. I've never felt more spiritually aware and connected to humanity than when I was pregnant. "

Her words resonate with me, that this can be a time for spiritual growth in my relationship with God as I join Him in the creative act of pregnancy. Then I hear my stomach rumble. Loudly. Rarity laughs, and I join her, embarrassed.

"Let's go get you something to eat. Your body

needs all the fuel it can get. Anything that you're craving?"

"Yeah, can we go to this Pho place? They have great chicken fried rice." I can practically taste it already.

"Say less. Let me text Brian and he can take us."

~

When I get to bed, after going through the motions of brushing my teeth and tying my hair, I feel a slight ache that seems to become more painful with every passing second. It was a gorgeous day, a delightful distraction from the reality of returning to school. Where I might run into Shane.

The thought of seeing him infuriates me and then scares the crap out of me, which then infuriates me more. The thing is, I'll have to see him, eventually. It's not like I can just avoid campus. When I see him again, I'll have to be cold and hard. It's the only way I'll be able to stop myself from melting when I see him. Because I still love him, and I can't just turn that off.

I sigh and close my eyes to see his brown ones looking into mine. I try to shake the image of his face from my mind, but it doesn't work.

Sweet dreams? Yeah, right. More like bittersweet ones.

I'm waiting at the finish line with a trophy in my hand as the runners round the corner. Shane is one of them, but there's another guy right at his heel. Even though they're still a suitable distance away, I can hear the footsteps. Wait, that makes no sense unless I'm actually hearing footsteps right now.

I open my eyes, now awake, and then listen to see

if I still hear them or if they were a figment of my imagination.

Nope, they're still there. I reach for my phone under my pillow to check the time. It's nearly 2 AM. Huh. Maybe Rarity is up using the bathroom or something. Wait, she has her own washroom in her room. Why would she be in the hallway?

She wouldn't.

As I pay closer attention, I notice the steps are heavy - as if they belong to a man. Did someone break in?

The footsteps stop. It seems like the man is outside my door. I hear the turning of the doorknob to enter my room.

Okay, time to get ready to ambush this guy. I make my body still as he draws near. When I feel a body bend over toward the bed and a hand touch the sheet, I spring into action.

I lift my leg to hit his nose with my knee. He grabs his bleeding nose with his left hand. Before he can recover, I grab his right arm and twist it, using the momentum of his body to spin him so that his back is toward me. Then I jump on his back and tackle him to the floor. I shove my knee into his back to keep him in place as I yell out for Rarity.

"Rare. Someone has broken in! Call the police!"

Then I return my attention to the man under my body. "Who are you, and what are you doing here?"

"Funny, I was wondering the same thing about you!" Oh great, a smart-aleck.

Before I can reply, Rarity bursts into the room with a fire extinguisher in her hands and a fierce look on her face until she sees the man. Then she laughs.

Laughs?

"Thia! That's my younger brother, Roderick! In all that's happened over the past few days, I totally forgot that he was supposed to visit."

Oh. How embarrassing. I get off his back and go to sit on the bed while Rarity turns on the light.

She offers him a hand to get off the floor. "Rod, what the heck? Why would you come in the middle of the night?"

"Why would I expect a random woman in the guest room bed?"

"Touché, little bro. Touché." She gives him an affectionate hug.

"Well, let me do the introductions. Rod, this Ruthia. Thia, this is Roderick." She gestures to each of us when she says our names.

He turns to face me, and I get a good look at him.

He's darker than Rarity, closer to my shade, with dark brown curly hair. And his eyes are more hazel than pure green. His face is handsome, even with a bloody nose.

I stand up, thanking God that I went to sleep in my jogging clothes, so I am wearing a bra.

"Hi Roderick, I'm sorry about earlier and your nose," I offer my hand for a handshake. His warm, firm hands enveloped mine, a comforting presence.

"All's forgiven, Ruthia." And I can tell by the look in his eyes that he's sincere.

"Well, now that we have that settled, let me set you up on the couch. It folds out into a bed, so it should still be pretty comfortable." Rarity moves to the door.

"I feel awful for displacing you. Maybe I should

take the couch."

"Absolutely not." They respond at the same time.

I put up my hands in surrender. "Okay, okay. I see the hospitality. I will keep the guest room."

"Consider it your room for as long as you need it." I have to command my eyes not to tear up at Rarity's words. She grabs sheets and a comforter from her linen closet and then we follow her into the living room. Roderick takes the lead in setting up his bed.

"Okay, Thia, remember we're going for a jog in a few hours." She yawns. "Rod, I love you, but we'll catch up another time when it's not time for me to sleep."

"No problem, get some rest, sis. I'll see you later this morning." He gives her a quick hug.

She walks away and now I'm just standing here, still embarrassed about earlier.

"Well, um, I'm sorry again for before!" I cough to cover up the squeaky tone of my voice.

He gives me a warm smile and my awkwardness eases up. "Water under the bridge. Would you like some tea?"

I nod, and we head to the kitchen. I go to fill and turn on the kettle while he grabs us two mugs and coasters. Our movements are like a choreographed dance. After placing them on the breakfast bar, he goes to the tea bags. He glances at me with an eyebrow raised.

"Mint," I answer his silent question, and he nods. I go to sit on one of the breakfast bar chairs, and he sits beside me once the water is hot and in our mugs.

"So, Ruthia, where did you learn the moves that you put on me earlier?"

I feel my cheeks warm and thank God that I'm too dark for a blush to show on my face. "In middle school, I took MMA and self-defense classes."

"That's great. Was this self-initiated or your parents' idea?"

"Parents. My mom has been sexually assaulted before, and she wanted me to defend myself so that I wouldn't have the same experience." It breaks my heart what she went through.

"That's terrible." We let a moment of silence pass. "Believe me, those classes were a success!"

"I'm so glad that my moves met your expert approval."

He chuckles at my teasing. "Well, I'm in the army. I don't think that makes me an expert, but I am professionally trained for combat."

"That's amazing! Thank you for choosing to serve our country this way."

"I have served no one yet. I'm still a student."

"Still, I appreciate the sacrifices that you're going to make." Then something hits me. "Wait!" I remember that it's the middle of the night and lower my voice. "You could've easily fended me off earlier. Why didn't you?"

"If I felt I was in any danger, I would have reacted appropriately. But I was underneath a beautiful woman. Why would I have wanted to move?"

Welp. I was not expecting that response. Was he flirting with me?

"Fam, the lights were off. You did not know if I was beautiful or not." I quickly drain my mug. "Well, I should go back to bed. I've got that jog with Rare and all." I grasp at this excuse to exit the premises.

He gasps. "But we've barely gotten to know each other. How am I supposed to know that you're not a psychopath waiting for the right moment to kill my sister and niece?" What he said is so ridiculous that I snort in laughter.

He laughs in response.

"Well, Cynthia is the reason I met Rarity, and I'd say she's an excellent judge of character."

He looks surprised. "Curiouser and curiouser."

"What is that supposed to mean exactly?"

"That I'm going to have a lot of fun getting to know you." He leans on the breakfast bar and props his head on his arm. His hazel eyes study my face with such intensity, giving weight to his words.

I try to bring back some levity to the conversation. "Oh really? And when will there be time for that?"

"Tomorrow, or rather today, if you're not busy?" I consider his easy invitation.

"I'm having breakfast with a friend, but I should be free around noon." I offer, and he smiles.

"Consider the rest of your day booked."

"Hmmm, that's hours of quality learning for you in exchange for what? You'd have to make this worth my while." My teasing earns me another laugh.

"I can promise you the best ice cream you'll ever have in your li-"

"Stop right there. You had me at ice cream."

He smiles at my interruption. "Well then, let's exchange numbers so that you can let me know where to pick you up."

I nod in agreement, and we exchange phones,

each adding our number. As he gives me back my phone, he holds my hand for a moment.

"I'm looking forward to our time together." There it is again, that serious voice, the intense look in his eyes. His beautiful hazel eyes.

"Good night, Rick," I whisper.

"A nickname already? Well, then, good night Nin." I raise an eyebrow. "Short for Ninja." I nod in approval.

"I like it. And at the risk of having to repeat our goodbyes again, I'll take my leave."

I walk back to my room with a smile on my face and when I close my eyes to sleep, I see hazel eyes instead of dark brown.

Chapter 7

My leg shakes as I sit on a bench outside of
IHOP, waiting for Rick to arrive. Gaelle's caution
during our breakfast rings through my mind.

"Sis, be careful. Your heart's in a delicate place.
Don't let yourself do things you wouldn't otherwise do
if things were normal."

She's right. The flirting last night was fun and
flattering, but it was also somewhat irresponsible. I'm
in no condition to be entering into anything romantic.
Not just because I don't want to rebound but also
because I have another human to consider. My child. I
hear my name and startle.

"Oops. I didn't mean to scare you." Rick gives me
an apologetic smile.

"No worries, I was just lost in thought."

He looks even more attractive than he did last
night, his tan leather jacket setting off his eyes in
ways that give me butterflies. I stand to get up, but I
don't know how to greet him. Do I give him a hug,
shake his hand? What?

I'm so awkward.

He saves me by gesturing to his car, a dark blue

Honda Pilot. "Care to get going?" I nod and head toward the passenger side of the car. He goes ahead of me, opening the door for me.

Why does he have to be chivalrous? I'm a sucker for these kinds of things. "Thanks." He gets in on his side, but before he turns the car on to drive off, he pauses and turns toward me.

"Nin, before we set out, I just want to apologize for last night."

My eyebrows raise in surprise.

"I fell into an old habit of flirting when I'm with a beautiful woman, which is something that I've been trying to break. I've been trying to hold off on showing romantic interest to someone until I get to know them more, but I forgot about that when we met, and I think I may have gotten a little intense. I just want to take any pressure off of our time together today and consider it an outing between friends. How do you feel about that?"

I instantly relax and sigh in relief. "That sounds great to me. Honestly, I just went through a breakup, like, two days ago, so I'm in no shape to be anything other than friends."

"Oh wow, thanks for sharing that with me. I'm glad that we're on the same page." He looks as grateful as I feel.

"Now, onto the fun part. Ice cream." I laugh at his excitement as he puts the key in the ignition and begins to pull out of his parking spot.

"I'm curious. What made you want to change your flirting habit?" I ask as we exit the plaza and get onto a main road.

"Well, I became a Christian about 7 months ago.

And that's changed everything about my life and how I want to approach things and people."

He glances at me, gauging my reaction. I give him a big smile. Any remaining nerves fade away. "That's amazing! Welcome to the family! I'm a believer as well."

"Really? That's awesome! I would love to hear your testimony. How did you come to know and follow Jesus?"

"I would love to hear yours, too."

He nods. "I'll share but ladies first." He teases, making me laugh.

"Okay, but then you're sharing yours, Rick. Deal?"

"Deal."

"Well, I grew up surrounded by Christianity as my dad is a pastor and my mom is a devout follower of Jesus. I always heard about God and His love, but I thought I had to do all the right things for it to be given to me."

He shakes his head.

"I know, not true, but it is what I believed. Then, when I was thirteen, I went to a youth camp run by our denomination during Christmas break. We were going to be working through Ephesians during that week. The first message wrecked me. When he broke down that God had loved and chosen us before He'd even made the world? That blew my mind. Holy Spirit helped me realize it wasn't at all about what I did, but God's decision to love me. I would say that I understood and believed the gospel that night. And the rest of the week, God taught me more and more about His love, grace, and power." Tears spring to my eyes as I remember that transforming week.

"That's beautiful, Nin. Thanks for sharing that with me." He sounds choked up, too. "I love hearing these stories of how God uniquely brings people into the Kingdom."

"Facts. Other people's testimonies always just make me love God more. Speaking of, I believe someone has a testimony debt to pay."

He shakes his head. "Nah, don't you know, Nin, that Jesus paid it all? I have no debt."

I laugh in response, "Right, that's what I should tell OSAP, that Jesus paid off every single kind of debt there is."

At this, he snorts. "Or you could just join the military and have your education paid for you." His voice is smug.

"Wow, way to rub it in my face! Not everyone can pass basic training, okay?"

He laughs. "Sounds like there's a deep wound there, Nin. You should get that checked out by the Holy Spirit."

"Don't declare illness over me. Don't you know that by his stripes we are healed?" I fail at keeping a serious face. He's laughing hard now.

"Touché. My bad theology has been matched by yours. We're even." My laughter dies off into a content smile. We're silent for a moment, and then I clear my throat.

"So, your story now, please?"

"You've been very patient. Well, I don't know if Rare told you we grew up in the church?" I nod and he continues. "Well, our parents modelled to us that we just need to do good things and live moral lives.

As I grew older into my teens, I came to realize that I didn't need religion for that. I could be moral on my own. Once I got into university, I decided that I was a humanist."

"This might be a dumb question, but what is a humanist?"

"Not a dumb question. There are many definitions, but for me, it looked like believing that reason and the scientific method are the only ways to discover what's true, that there is no supernatural aspect to the world, and that everyone can live however they want as free beings as long as they're not hurting anyone else. Does that make sense?"

I nod. It made sense, but it sounded like an empty way to live.

"But then, at the end of my third year, while I was working on a paper, two random people came up to me and asked if I would share my perspective on life with them. They had these cards with common worldview answers to different big questions, and I would just have to choose which cards resonated with me. It seemed like an excellent distraction from my paper, so I let them sit with me, and we did the activity. It was hard because I knew what cards humanism would lead me to pick, but I realized that those weren't always what resonated. It hit me that my worldview had a lot of gaps.

"They asked if one of them, Doug, could share their Christian perspective with me, and I said yes. My upbringing allowed me to predict Doug's card choices, but one surprised me. In the question of where one finds moral and spiritual truth, he chose the Bible and reason. Doug explained that reason led him to believe the Bible to be true and that for him, believing in Jesus was logical. I had heard no one say that before, and I wanted to understand what he meant. From then on, Doug and I became friends..."

My ringing phone interrupts him. I glance down to see who it is. Shane again. I quickly decline the call and then put my phone on silent. "I'm so sorry about that! Please continue."

"No worries." The smile he gives me shows he means it. "So, over the spring and summer, he journeyed with me by helping me come to the plausibility of God's existence, then examining the claims of different religions, and finally reading about Jesus in the Bible. Jesus captivated me with how unique, wise, and loving He was. I came to believe that He was worth following, and it's the best decision I've ever made. I'm still fairly new to the faith, but I've grown a lot by going to the Bible studies and prayer meetings that are run by the Christian club that Doug was involved in and have even gone out to do perspectives with random people too! It's been amazing to learn more about Jesus and begin to share him with people in my life. Anyway, I've been talking for a while. I'll shut up now."

"Are you kidding? I loved hearing your story. In different parts, I got chills at how God led you to faith in Him. Praise God!" My enthusiasm makes him smile. "I even wish I could be that bold about my faith. I've always been super scared of sharing what I believe with people, partly because I don't know how. I would love to see those cards you mentioned."

"Yeah, for sure! I always carry a pack with me to always be ready. I'll show you them when we get to where we're going."

"Sweet! Thank you. Have you been able to share your faith with Rarity?"

"I've tried, but I think it's hard for her to take me seriously as her little brother." He says, his voice sad.

"That's hard. Well, I want you to know that God is pursuing your sister. He told me He wants me to show her what faith in Jesus can look like. Gaelle, that's the friend I was at IHOP with, and I are praying for her salvation."

He wipes away tears from his eyes. "That's such an answered prayer, for real. I'm so glad that God brought you into her life. Wait, how did you guys meet? You said Cynthia was involved?"

I sighed. I knew I would have to share about my current situation, but I'd been dreading it because I didn't want him to treat me differently.

"That was a heavy sigh. It sounds like you might need some ice cream in your system before sharing?"

I nod, grateful for his sensitivity. "Thanks for giving me time."

"No problem. We're almost there, anyway. Have you heard of Kawartha Dairy?"

I shake my head.

"It's a Canadian company that produces all things dairy. Their locations are all more up north, but it's definitely worth the gas money. Trust me. We're still a little way away from the closest location in Newmarket. Would you like to get something to eat beforehand? There's a great burger place owned by Christians that we can visit if you're down."

"Sure. It feels like ages ago that I had my pancakes. Gaelle and I usually talk for at least an hour or so after we're done eating. We always tip well though, so the waitstaff don't hate us."

He laughs. "She sounds like a great friend. Tell me about her. How did you meet?"

"Well, our churches are in the same church network. So, from when we were small, we would be at the same conferences and conventions, and we also lived in the same city. My family wasn't too keen on me going on playdates or sleepovers, very Jamaican of them, but her family was the exception. We're both only children, so she's always felt like a sister to me. She's always down to pray for me and we've regularly done devotionals together. I couldn't imagine my life without her, to be honest."

He nods. "That's amazing, Nin. It's how I feel about Doug. We've just passed a year of friendship, but I'm hoping we will stay friends for a lifetime. I couldn't ask for a better brother. Also, we're here." He turns into a plaza.

I hadn't even realized that we'd come off the highway, so engrossed in our conversation.

As soon as we get in, I fall in love with the joint. One wall is filled with a scripture passages, and there are a bunch of Catholic/Christian-themed puns on the menu. "This is great!"

"Wait till you try their burgers."

We order and head to an empty table to wait for our food. It's not long before our burgers are ready. "Mind if I pray for our food before we dig in?"

I nod in assent, touched by his request.

"Heavenly Father, thanks for drawing us both to yourself. We came to you in different ways, but we worship and follow the same God and each have the same Spirit. What a miracle. Bless this food and the hands that prepared it, and our time together. Amen."

"Amen."

I eagerly take a bite out of my burger and inadvertently moan. "Mercy. This is good. I now trust your judgement on food and have more expectations for the ice cream."

"Wow, you couldn't take my word for it, eh? You believe because you have tasted, but blessed is the one who believes and has not tasted."

I laugh at his misquote of scripture. "Don't make me laugh too much or I might choke on my food."

"Okay, okay. I'll lay aside my comedic prowess until we're back on the highway."

I shake my head, laughing at his drama. But he keeps his word, remaining quiet. We enjoy a peaceful silence as we eat, and it gives me time to think about how I'm feeling. My heart is all over the place.

Other than the initial awkwardness when he picked me up, I have felt safe and comfortable. I've also laughed so much. Roderick is shaping up to be a great friend. But he also is a likely candidate for a crush. I recognize the romantic feelings beginning because it's the same way I used to feel around Shane.

This is dangerous territory.

'Father,' I silently pray, *'thank You for giving me awareness of my feelings. Now, I will give them to You. Help me relate to your son as a sister. Amen.'*

I finish my burger and notice that he's wrapping up, too. Without speaking, he raises his eyebrow in question as he gestures toward my tray. I nod, and he goes to throw out our wrappers and return our trays.

And then we're off, back to our ice cream

adventure.

"How do you feel about enjoying some music for the rest of our drive? This band I like just released a new album that I haven't listened to yet."

"Sounds good. I'm game."

Soon, music is playing. The vibe is very Imagine Dragons, but the lyrics are about the Christian faith. I'm into it and make mental notes of songs that I enjoy listening to again later.

It feels like no time has passed when I notice we are coming off the highway again and turning into another plaza. Before long, we are at the counter ordering our ice cream.

"I'll take a scoop of coconut and a scoop of sugar shock maple in a cup please," I order, giddy. These are flavors I have yet to see anywhere else. I go to grab my wallet from my jacket pocket, but Rick stops me, placing a hand on my arm.

"I've got this. Let me treat you in this way." I search his face to see if he is serious or if I should protest.

"Okay, thank you."

"Thank you for letting me do this."

The guy ringing up our order clears his throat, and we glance at him to see an amused expression on his face.

"Right, can you remind me of what is the difference between regular chocolate and death by chocolate?" Rick asks.

"Death by Chocolate has dark chocolate chunks and chocolate sauce. It's chocolate on steroids. Clearly, you love chocolate, so you should get it." He says the last part knowingly.

Rick and I exchange a confused glance. How could this guy know what Rick did or didn't like? He just met us now. And then realization dawns.

I am the chocolate that Rick supposedly loves.

Before I can respond, Rick speaks up. "I'm going to assume that you are an ice cream psychic and didn't just compare a human being to a dessert." His voice is firm, with an undercurrent of anger.

"Whoa man, it was a joke. Chill out."

"Dehumanizing someone by reducing them to their race and then reducing their race to food is not funny. You're lucky I promised her great ice cream and that I respect the family who owns this business, otherwise I would already be out of here. I'll take two scoops of the 'death by chocolate'." Though his voice is calm, I can see the anger in his eyes. They look like a forest storm, brown and green colliding with each other.

The guy doesn't speak again as Rick pays and we get our ice cream. Since the weather is warm for an April Saturday, we decide to eat at a picnic table outside and sit on the same side.

"Ruthia, I am so sorry about that guy in there." I can see that his body is tense, still upset about what happened.

"Not your fault. Ice cream sellers are not immune from ignorance."

"Ignorance is right. It was just so disrespectful, on multiple levels." I let him vent, and he relaxes as he lets off steam.

"I appreciate how you responded, though. You were firm and clear without being mean or full of rage. Thank you for that." I see him relax more as a result of my words.

"Praise God, that was the Holy Spirit. I've been asking Him to help me work on my anger. My dad was a very angry man. We never felt safe around him, especially when he would drink alcohol. I don't want to be like that. I never want people to fear me that way." He lowers his head.

"Hey, Roderick. Look at me." He lifts his head slightly to meet my gaze. "Thanks for trusting me with that part of your family story, Rick. Seriously, I'm honored." His smile returns to his face, and it's like watching a sunrise.

"Well, I promised you great ice cream, and I'll break it if I keep talking, since the ice cream is already melting."

It's as good as he promised.

"Okay, this was definitely worth the subtle racism. Wow."

He laughs. "You're not wrong. But next time, I'll go to another location."

"You'll have to take me with you. I never knew that coconut and maple could taste so good! It's like a perfect mix of my two ethnic identities, Jamaican and Canadian."

"Ayy. You're Caribbean background? That's great! My mom is Afro-Trinidadian."

"I didn't know that! No wonder Rare and I get along so well!"

"I'm surprised you didn't know about our family. Now, I need to know how you came to be living with my sister."

"That's fair. Just let me finish my ice cream first?" He lets me stall.

"Okay. Let's just enjoy the ice cream."

I try to eat as slowly as possible, partly because I want to savor the flavors, but mostly to delay having to share. Alas, my cup is empty, and it's time for me to share.

"Well, do you remember how I said that I'm just coming off of a breakup? The breakup happened because I'm pregnant." I pause and glance at his face. He looks surprised.

"And your ex was the father?" He clarifies, and I nod. "What a waste yute!"

I burst out in laughter at his angry outburst.

"I'm serious, Nin. And he's a believer?" He clarifies further, and I nod again. "Wow. So shameful, not taking responsibility for his actions. Okay, I'll let you keep talking."

I'm surprised that he hasn't commented on me being pregnant, and it's evidence that I sinned sexually.

"Well, after he broke up with me. I had decided to get an abortion."

He gasps.

"It's something that I never thought I'd ever do, as I believe the Bible is pro-life. But there I was, all the same. The abortion clinic I was going to happens to be near Cynthia's daycare. I ended up falling on one of her toys, and then she pulled me into her daycare room. It was a Mommy and Me day, but Rare hadn't been able to make it. Cynthia asked me to be her stand-in mommy. Through Cynthia, God showed me He wanted me to be a mother and that I needed to keep this baby. When Rare came to pick up Cynthia, we met and spent the afternoon together. So, yeah, that's how we met."

"Wow. There's so much there, but I still don't know how you ended up living with Rarity and Cynthia."

"Welp. I thought you would not catch that. So, since I kept the baby, I knew I had to tell my parents. They treated me like an adult even though I still lived with them, and I knew I would need their help with all of this. My dad flipped out." At this part, I draw up my legs so that my head can comfortably fit in between my knees. "He wanted to know who the father was. And well, I had never seen him so unhinged. I felt like I would put Shane in danger by revealing his identity, so I refused. This led to him kicking me out of the house."

"Am I remembering correctly that your dad is a pastor?"

"Yes, you are."

"Jeeze, okay. Keep going."

"Well, earlier that day, Rare had said that she would be happy to help me in any way I needed. When I got into the taxi, I just said Rare's address. And she was kind enough to take me in and care for me these past couple of days. And here we are." I stare straight ahead. I didn't want to see his reaction to all of this information. Shane's face looked horrified. My dad had looked disgusted. How would Roderick look?

"Nin, would you look at me?" I sigh and turn to face him.

All I see is compassion.

"I don't even know what to respond to first." He starts off. "First of all, I'm so glad that you're keeping the baby. Second of all, the men in your life suck, except for me." At this, I snort, and he looks happy to see that he made me smile. "And third of all, you have to be one of the strongest people I know. You're going through so much loss; losing a serious relationship - well, that's an assumption, but I don't think you would've slipped up sexually if you guys had just started dating, am I right?" I nod. "Right, so losing that then losing your home and in all of this losing the future you probably thought you'd have. And yet, you still trust in God. I'm in awe of God at work in you, Ruthia."

I don't know if it's the sincerity in his voice or his words that do it, but I end up bursting into tears. Up to this point, only women have been this kind to me. I didn't realize how much it would mean for me for a man to not judge me.

He tentatively places his hand on my back and slowly rubs it in circles. Without thinking, I lean into him, and he wraps one of his arms around me.

"Do you mind if I pray for you, Nin?"

All I can do is nod.

"Father, we come to you now in raw and vulnerable places. Thank You for keeping Ruthia. Thank You for bringing her this far. Thank You for keeping her heart soft to You. Lord, would You bless this pregnancy to be healthy. Lord, would you provide for all of Ruthia's needs? Lord, would this baby grow to know you and love you when they grow up? In Jesus' name, we pray, amen."

"Amen," I whisper and use the sleeve of my cardigan to dry my face.

"Well, how about we get home, eh?" The

gentleness in his voice nearly sends me back into tears. These pregnancy hormones are no joke.

"That sounds like a good idea to me."

Chapter 8

As Gaelle and I walk into the waiting room area, my chest tightens and my breaths become more and more shallow. I can't help it. This is the first ultrasound, and I'm terrified. What if the baby isn't alive anymore? What if the technician is really cold? What if they have to do an inner probe instead of just on the belly?

I should've left Google alone last night.

"Sis, breathe. It's all going to be okay." She whispers to me and then takes my hand. I lean my head on her shoulder and try to take deep breaths. It doesn't work, but her presence with me is a blessing.

We walk toward the receptionist's desk.

"Health card and requisition?" Her voice is curt. I reach into my pocket for it and give it to her. Her demeanor does nothing good for my nerves.

"Great. Now fill out this form and bring it back to me when you're done. The ultrasound technician will call your name when it's your turn."

I nod as Gaelle takes the clipboard from the receptionist. We find two chairs, and I go to work filling out the form. I'm too anxious to even read what

I'm signing. When I'm done, Gaelle takes it back to the receptionist. I bend over to put my head in between my legs and try to deep breathe again. I hear Gaelle return and sit in the chair to my left. She rubs circles onto my back, and my body slowly relaxes.

"Thia, I've got something funny to share with you. You'll laugh, I promise." She tugs on my left arm so that I'll sit up.

"Okay, I'm all ears."

"The receptionist thinks that we're a couple."

"A couple of what?"

And then Gaelle laughs. "A couple, as in being in a romantic relationship."

Before I can help it, I snort, and Gaelle laughs more. "How do you know this?"

"When I brought back the form, she was like 'It looks like your partner is really nervous. I think what you two are doing is beautiful. Don't worry, you'll be able to go in with her.' I was going to correct her but then, would I still be allowed to go in and support you? Probably not."

I shake my head, laughing at her very Gaelle thought process.

"Normally, I wouldn't want you to practice deceit, but I don't think I can do this by myself," I admit.

"Let's chalk this up to being a Rahab lie, deceit for the greater good." I smile at her. This girl, she's the best.

"Ruthia Walkins?" I hear my name called to the right of me and turn to see a woman in a white lab coat and a mask gesturing for me to follow her. I wipe the sweat off my hands on my jeans and get up. Gaelle grabs my hand and then winks at me, making me laugh.

We follow the technician into a dark room. I see a computer, a desk chair, a hospital-like bed, and another chair.

"So, I'll give you a couple of minutes to take off your pants and underwear. You can use the paper towel on the bed to cover up your lower half and then just lie down on the bed."

I nod at her instructions, trying to hide how panicked I am. Once she leaves the room, Gaelle pulls me into a hug.

"Match my breathing, Thia, match my breathing." I quiet myself to hear her breaths and try to follow their pattern. The panic subsides a bit. I pull back and then follow the tech's instructions.

Pretty soon, I'm on the examination bed with the paper towels covering my nether region, and then I hear a knock at the door. "Come in," Gaelle calls out, and the tech does just that.

She sits in the desk chair and types away on her computer keyboard. Then I see her pour a gel-like substance onto a probe.

"Okay, I'm going to pull back the paper towels a bit so that we can get a good look at what's happening inside of you. The gel might feel cold."

Though I can't see her face, her voice is warm, and that eases away a little more of the panic.

I nod in consent, and she does exactly what she said. The gel is cool on my skin, but pleasantly so. Like a breeze on a humid day. A refreshing coolness.

As she moves the probe around, I hear a whooshing sound and see a grey-scale image on the computer screen. It looks like a large empty black space, and then I see the littlest peanut-shaped blob in the sac. The tech taps away at her keyboard, and we zoom on the blob.

"There's the baby."

As I see the little blob move back and forth, tears come to my eyes. I glance at Gaelle, and tears are already streaming down her face.

"First pregnancy?" I nod, too overcome with emotion to speak.

"Well, your baby has a nice and strong heartbeat. Listen." And then she clicks away at the screen and a strong pitter patter echoes throughout the room. As soon as I hear their heartbeat, my own steadies.

I feel an awe saturated in peace, a love that I didn't even know I was capable of and something else, hope. There is a brand-new life inside of me! What a freaking miracle!

She taps away, and I no longer hear my baby. It feels like such a loss. I expect the peace I felt to vanish as well, but it doesn't.

"I just have to get some measurements done to determine how far along you are and your due date. You can continue to watch your baby on the screen, though."

"Thank you so much,"

Time escapes me as I look at my baby. I'm captivated. All too soon, or so it feels, the tech removes the probe from my body and the image on the screen disappears.

"Alright, we're all done. Let me print off a photo for you. I will send the results to the doctor who ordered your ultrasound, and they'll walk you through your next few steps."

Then she hands me a small black-and-white photo of my baby and how far along I am.

"Thank you so much!"

"You're welcome. I'll leave now to give you some privacy. You can use as much paper towel as you need to clean off the gel." With a wave goodbye to Gaelle, she exits the room.

I hand the photo to Gaelle and then wipe off the ultrasound goo. I slip back into my skirt and then we're off. Once we're outside the ultrasound clinic, Gaelle breaks the silence. "That was amazing!"

"It really was. It just made it all so real and so worth everything that's already happened. I'm so glad that I got such a nice technician."

"An angel in disguise." Gaelle has always believed that angels are among us for specific help when we need it.

Once we're back in her car, we look at the photo again together.

"You okay if I take a picture of this on my phone?"

"That's actually a genius idea! Go ahead. I'm going to do the same."

Following our photo-taking, we drive back to Rarity's, stopping at a Five Guys on the way. I'm feeling for a quality burger.

As we walk into the condominium, it hits me how wild it is that it has become home to me.

We settle at the breakfast bar, pray, and then dig into our food. This hit the spot. We enjoy a comfortable silence as we eat.

"Thank you for letting me join you today, Thia."

"Are you kidding? Thank you for agreeing to come with me. I couldn't have done it alone." She leans her head on my shoulder, and I lean into her as well, a quasi-hug since our hands are greasy from the delicious burgers.

"It made scripture come alive for me, like in Psalm 139, when it talks about God forming babies in the womb. It was wild to actually see that on the screen."

I nod in agreement. "Yeah, Jeremiah 1 also comes to mind. How this baby is already set apart and chosen for a special purpose."

"Amen, girl, you better preach!" I roll my eyes at her teasing but still laugh with her. "For real though, I'm excited about this little life and all God has in store for him or her and for you, Thia. You might think this has disrupted God's call on your life or detoured your destiny, but we're not off God's plan. You are right in his will."

I blink away the threat of tears. "Thanks, Elle. I needed that encouragement. I'm feeling really anxious about whether I'll be a good enough mom and will actually be able to show this baby what Jesus is like and how worthy He is of our lives."

"That desire shows you're on the right track. Actually, let's pray right now." I nod at her suggestion.

"Heavenly Father, Thank You for today. Thank You for the ultrasound technician You gave us, bless her Lord. Thank You for the life and health of this baby. We look forward with anticipation and expectancy to what You have planned for this little one and Ruthia. Lord, we know there's an anointing on Thia to love children. Would this child get the first fruits of that? Lord, would You give Thia peace and confidence that You will provide everything she needs, practically and spiritually? We bless this pregnancy and declare Your glory in it all. In Jesus's Name, amen."

"Amen. That was beautiful."

We both open our eyes and glance toward the voice that said those words. Roderick with Rarity and Cynthia.

"We didn't realize we had an audience," Gaelle wipes her hands with a napkin and gets off from her stool. "I believe we have yet to meet. My name is Gaelle." She holds out her hand for a handshake.

"Roderick. Nice to meet you." They exchange smiles, and I feel something weird in my stomach.

"Hey guys!" I say and wave, ignoring the feeling. Hopefully, it's not my body disagreeing with the burger.

"Who were you talking to, Tante Gaelle?" Cynthia asks.

Gaelle squats down to Cynthia's height. "I was talking to God."

"Oh! Uncle Roderick knows who God is. I've heard him talk to God before, too. But how do you know God is listening if you can't see God?"

"That's faith, lil' Thia. That means we trust God is real even though we cannot see Him." Roderick explains, stooping down too before answering. He and Gaelle, now also on the same level, exchange smiles again. And again, there's that feeling. A slight tightness in my chest, like the beginning of an anxiety attack, mixed with a feeling of unease in my belly, like I'm going to throw up.

Crap. I think I'm jealous. Why am I jealous though? Rick and I are just friends, and I just got out of a relationship. I know I still love Shane. Is it possible to love him and like someone else at the same time?

"Thia?" I hear Gaelle say my name, not even realizing that I'd been missing the conversation.

"Sorry, mom brain. What did you say?"

"No worries, just saying that I'm going to head home and work on a paper unless you need anything else?"

My best friend is so kind, helpful, and beautiful! No wonder Roderick would like her. And he's a great guy! I should be happy that they are vibing.

Should being the operative word.

I realize that I've zoned out again, but blink myself back to the present moment. "Yeah, I am good. Thanks for everything today. You're the best." I say, and I mean it. I love her so much and don't know how I would process all that's taken place without her. I get up to give her a hug.

"Alright, sis! It's been great meeting you." Rick waves to her. She waves back at all of us.

"Bye, fam!"

Sis. Fam. Maybe their vibe was more sibling-esque, not romantic. My body relaxes and then I shake my head at myself. I've got to get a grip on myself and my emotions.

I return to the breakfast bar and gather the packaging to throw it in the garbage.

"Five Guys? I love that place! You guys have good taste in burgers. I always feel like I was meant to be their sixth guy." I snort at his dad joke. He can be such a dork sometimes.

Lord knows I have a thing for dorks.

"Yeah, it was great. But I'm going to follow Gaelle's lead and finish a paper that I have due as well. I'll see you in the morning for our run, Rare. Night, Rick. Good night, Thia."

After saying my goodbyes, I rush to my room. I can't leave their presence fast enough. I need to be alone with these thoughts and feelings and figure them out.

"Lord. I need You. Give me clarity. Give me peace. Help me walk in Your way. Sanctify my emotions, and set them apart for You. Would they not lead me, but would You lead them, Holy Spirit? In Jesus's Name, amen."

I feel slightly better after praying, but only slightly. Frustrated, I head over to my backpack and pull out my laptop. Maybe I can at least make some headway on something tonight.

Chapter 9

My phone has been burning in my pocket all day. I'm unbearably aware of it while avoiding it at the same time. Shane has WhatsApped me a video. From the thumbnail, it's a video of himself.

It was painful enough just to open our chat and see our most recent messages, all cute and lovey-dovey. That Ruthia was so confidently in love. She didn't know what was coming for her.

I'm tempted to just delete it, but I can't. Curiosity bids me to watch it. Distrust cautions me against doing so.

And so here I am, lying on my bed, proofreading my paper. Or attempting to. My attention continues to drift to my phone.

This is so tiring.

Let's just get this done. I can hear curiosity's victory march as distrust shakes its head, knowing that it tried to warn me.

I take out my phone and open his message, then press play before I can change my mind.

There he is, in a simple black tee and maroon cardigan. The one I'd stolen from him early in our relationship. He looks too handsome for his own good. Who am I kidding? For my own good!

He clears his throat and then speaks. "Ruthia." Lord, help me. He says my name like it's special to him. Like he loves me.

"I love you." I pause the video. A few seconds in, I'm already overwhelmed. His earnest, forlorn gaze is captivating. You can't fake this look, but what does it mean? I take a deep breath and press play again.

"Ruthia, I made a terrible mistake in that Tim Hortons. I walked away from the love of my life and trampled on your trust. I am so sorry. Those words are inadequate to express the regret I feel at my behavior. I want you, Ruthia. I miss you. I forgot what life was like before you were back in my life. It's like watching a movie on a computer versus in IMAX. There's no comparing the two." I pause again.

He sounds like he means it. He looks like he means it. I don't think I've ever seen him look so sad. My heart feels like it's about to jump out of my chest. It wants to run to him. Every word he says stitches the punctures he'd made. I take another deep breath, trying to still my heart and press play again.

"I will do whatever it takes to have us back together again, Ruthia. I am determined to woo you if you'll let me." His face has taken on a determined look now. Oh boy. Assertive Shane is a whole vibe.

"I know you hate surprises," I laugh at this, "so I'm going to lay out the entire game plan. I want you to know what to expect." Now he looks nervous, borderline insecure.

"From my research, your pregnancy hinges on Thursdays. So, every Thursday, you will get a video from me. In it, I'll share what the milestones are for our baby and then pray for you two." Our baby. He says those two words with so much love.

"Every day, you will get a voice message at 7:16." For my birthday. "To honor one of the best days in history, your birthday. That message will be me sharing something I love about you, along with a picture of us." I don't know how much more my heart can take.

"And then, every Sunday, I will send to you a few books from Quinn Loftis to read for the week. Eventually, you'll have them all - just like you've been wanting for years." I squeal.

"Ruthia, I hope that I'll be able to remind you of how beautiful our relationship was and show you how much I love you. But I won't force myself on you." At this, he looks resigned.

"If you don't want me to do any of this, react to this message with a thumbs down and I'll back off." He surprised me. "If you don't do this, then I'll take it as you being open to giving me this opportunity. I promise you won't regret it." Then his eyes look directly into the camera, almost like he's looking at me, right in the eyes.

"I love you." So much feeling, so much weight that he's put into these three words.

"Now, onto our little one. You are 8 weeks now! You should have your first ultrasound soon, if you haven't already. This baby's heartbeat should be discernible. From what I've seen online, babies at this stage look similar to little peanuts! It's adorable. Also, their brain is developing neural pathways!" He looks so giddy. "You're experiencing nausea by now, maybe even vomiting." Now, his face is solemn. "I wish I could be there to hold your hair back or get you as much Chinese food as you want. I gave up the privilege of serving you. And I regret it, one hundred percent. Let me pray for you both now." I see him bow his head and close his eyes.

"Heavenly Father, thank You for the miracle You're doing in and with Thia. Help her persevere through the crappy early pregnancy symptoms. Give her grace to eat and enjoy food without nausea or vomiting. And Lord, bless this baby. Would their brain develop in the ways it needs to? And would, one day, they grow up to know and follow You. In Your Name, amen."

"Amen," I repeat. My heart is more moved and torn than ever before. Especially when he looks up and I see little tears at the corners of his eyes.

"Well, thanks for the time you've given to watching this video. I hope you give me a chance to show you that I mean my words. Grace and peace, I love you." He gives a little wave and then the video ends.

Dang it. This video was everything I love about him. His humor, his prayer life, his knowing of me. This is the man I fell in love with.

I miss him too.

I forward the video to Gaelle with "SOS." as a caption. I see both arrows appear and then they quickly turn blue. Good, she's seen it. Hopefully, she watches it immediately and can give me some counsel.

The minutes passing by feel like an eternity.

And then she calls.

"Elle! Help!"

"That was some video, Thia. I don't even know where to begin. It was like the Shane we knew and loved. How are you doing?"

I let out a nonsensical groan.

"Use your words, Thia. Let's process this."

I take a deep breath and just start blurting thoughts out.

"I love him so much, but he hurt me so much, and I want to trust him, but I don't know how, and I think I may also have a crush on Rick, which just makes this all even more confusing because it doesn't mean I love Shane any less, or does it? I don't even know! It may be easier to just give him a thumbs down and move on with my life, Rick in the picture or not, but is that even what's best for the baby? Shouldn't they have a family? I just don't know, Elle. I need to be told what to do. Please tell me what to do." It all comes out in a breath, and then I struggle to grab the next one, beginning to wheeze.

"Breathe, ma chère. Breathe. Inhale, exhale." She models deep breaths, and I try to follow her. The wheezing dwindles.

"Thank you, meilleure amie."

"Okay. Now, for some tough love." I brace myself. "I can't tell you what to do, but I will highlight three things. The first thing you said is that you love him. Present tense. The question is: do you love him enough to give him another chance?"

I nod and then remember that she can't see me. "I'm nodding," I inform her.

"Good, the second thing I'll say is that if you choose to give him that chance, you'll want to tell him to send the books to my place, since you're not living at home anymore."

"Facts. That totes slipped my mind."

"And lastly, while I can't tell you what to do, I know who can. Yahweh can tell you what to do, so I think you should spend some time with him."

I nod again, feeling chagrined. "What does it say about me since I texted you for advice before I prayed?"

"It means that you're in process, Thia. And that's okay. Can I pray for you, sis?"

I sigh in gratitude for the needed reminder and her offer of prayer. "Please do."

"Father, give Ruthia wisdom. Show her what to do. Make Your will clear. Help her heart to not lead her in circles, but have her heart led by You. You say that if we ask for wisdom, You'll give it if we are not double-minded. Give Ruthia an undivided heart, one that is solely focused on glorifying You. In Jesus's Name, amen."

"Amen. Thanks, best friend. I love you."

"I love you too. Now go spend that time with Jesus." Her voice is playfully stern, making me laugh.

"Yes, ma'am. Bye!" I hang up the call.

"Okay, Lord. I'm here. I want what You want. Speak to me, please." I try to quiet my heart to hear His voice, but it's radio silence. Like I'm only getting spiritual static.

I give it another few minutes and sigh. I'm definitely lacking the patience to be still and know that He is God. But then, I get an idea. I haven't done this recently, but maybe it's time.

Thankfully, my mom packed my physical Bible. I

get off the bed and grab it from my dresser, then kneel at my bedside. "Okay, Lord. I trust You are going to speak to me through Your Word." Then I close my eyes, run my fingers back and forth along the pages of my Bible and count to 16. Once I reach that, I pause my finger and open my eyes.

Hopefully, this worked.

I open my Bible to where my finger stopped and see that I landed on John 21.

I land on verse 15 and my heart feels at peace.

"When they had eaten breakfast, Jesus asked Simon Peter, "Simon, son of John, do you love me more than these?" "Yes, Lord," he said to him, "you know that I love you." "Feed my lambs," he told him. A second time he asked him, "Simon, son of John, do you love me?" "Yes, Lord," he said to him, "you know that I love you." "Shepherd, my sheep," he told him. He asked him the third time, "Simon, son of John, do you love me?" Peter was grieved that he asked him the third time, "Do you love me?" He said, "Lord, you know everything; you know that I love you." "Feed my sheep," Jesus said."

Peter had denied Jesus. And here, Jesus restores him. He allows Peter to affirm his love for Him. And then, he entrusts the ministry to Peter. First comes an opportunity for Peter to reaffirm his love, and then comes Jesus' expressing trust.

Like Jesus, I need to give Shane a chance to show his professed love. This can rebuild trust.

"I hear You, Lord. Loud and clear. Thank you for meeting me where I am. Thank you for speaking. Give me grace to be like You."

Then, before I can change my mind or lose my

godly confidence, I grab my phone and react to Shane's message with a thumbs up.

I get up to put my Bible away, and when I check my phone again, I have a message from Shane. It's a YouTube video of a Veggie Tales song from Jonah: 'God of Second Chances'. I laugh.

Instinctively, I react to it with a laughing emoji and then stop myself. Things felt so normal for a moment. But things aren't normal. There's a reason he needs a second chance after all.

Instead, I close the app and put my phone away. Maybe now I can actually proofread my paper.

Chapter 10

I try to keep my leg still as I sit in this semi-uncomfortable chair at Cinnabon. The nerves end up coming out through my fingers instead, drumming on the table in front of me. It's weird to feel nervous to see my mom, but it's even weirder that I haven't seen her in almost 2 weeks. With all that's been going on, I just haven't had the time for us to spend together. This is the longest either of us has ever spent away from each other.

The pressure builds in my chest as I check my phone for the umpteenth time and see that she's late.

Maybe she decided not to come?

Maybe she agrees with my dad and doesn't want me to be her daughter anymore?

Maybe - the thought stops as I see her round the corner. She notices me almost as soon as I see her and she gives me a big smile. My nerves disappear.

I'm safe.

I stand up to give her a hug and nearly fall backwards with the force of her embrace. She steps back, keeping her hands on my shoulders. She's assessing me, making sure that I am okay. I see her brown eyes get cloudy with tears as she cups the side of my face with one of her hands.

"My Bella. My Ruthie. How I've missed you." At her gentle touch and my childhood nickname, tears come to me as well.

"Momma," I haven't called her that in ages, and it prompts another hug. We stay like that for a long time. Almost like we're breathing each other in. I could not care less what anyone who sees us is thinking. I missed my mom so much, more than I'd even realized.

We break the hug, and she holds my hands, giving them the gentlest squeeze. "I'm going to get us some cinnamon buns, and then we can talk, okay?"

"Okay." My heart somehow feels both at rest and in pain at being with her again.

I don't have time to contemplate these paradoxical emotions because she comes with a plate in each hand. I get utensils and return to the table as she just finished settling in the other chair.

"Okay if I pray and then we can dig in while they're still warm?"

I nod in agreement.

"Father, thank you for keeping my daughter safe. Your daughter safe. Bless our time together, bless this food that we're about to eat, and bless the people who made it for us to enjoy. We love You. Thank You for loving us first. Amen."

"Amen."

It's a comfortable silence as we eat. Normally, I devour these things, but I choose to savour each bite. This feels like a pocket of unrushed time, of peace. We finish at about the same time and then relax in our seats.

"Okay, my love. How are you doing physically, emotionally, and spiritually?" I smile at her go-to question.

"Physically, I'm simultaneously super hungry and somewhat nauseous. Not the most fun combination, that's for sure." She nods in understanding.

"On the other fronts, things feel pretty messy and all tangled up."

"Let's see if we can tease them apart together, then. Let's start with how you feel about being a mother. How are you feeling in that respect?"

"I feel so humbled. I can't believe that God would entrust me with another person's life. Oh! That reminds me, I have something for you!" Her eyebrows raise in surprise as I dip my hand into my purse and feel around for my ultrasound picture. Ah, there it is.

"I had my ultrasound a week and a half ago and I thought you might like this picture, especially since I already have it saved on my phone." I hold out the small square paper toward her.

She handles it gingerly, as if it were the most delicate thing ever entrusted to her. "He or she is so beautiful. My grandchild." Her voice chokes up and she cries. I hand her a napkin, and she smiles in thanks.

"It's incredible, eh? But, I also feel anxious because there's so much uncertainty right now regarding what being a mom is going to look like; where I will live and whether I'll be a single mom. It's just a lot to navigate."

"You're right, it is a lot. What's happening with

the baby's dad? But, don't tell me his name. I don't think it's wise for your father to know, and I don't want to be put in a position where I'll be lying to him."

"Totes fair. Thanks for saying that. Well, I love him, Mom, and he wants to get back together with me…" I think of the daily texts I've been getting and the video that he sent yesterday morning. So sweet, so consistent, so the guy that I fell in love with. "But I just can't trust him anymore. Not after he walked out on me when I needed him."

"That's valid."

"Then there's also the fact that there's another guy."

"The plot thickens!" I laugh at her drama.

"He's the brother of the woman I'm staying with, and he loves the Lord. He's a great friend." I smile as I think about the rhythms we've adopted together.

From chatting in the mornings while Rarity takes Cynthia to daycare to sharing about our times in the Bible and what we're learning about God; it's been such a delight to have him in my life. My mind goes back to a few days ago.

~

"So, what did you read today? You're still in Ecclesiastes, right?" Roderick asks me and gulps down some water. He carries around this hefty 2-litre jug all day and he's about halfway already when it's only noon! We're chatting as I heat lunch for us, some Jamaican patties.

"Mhmm. Today I read Chapter 7. Verse 14 stood out to me. Let me pull out my phone to read it to you. I don't want to butcher it." I slide my phone out of my pocket and swipe around to my Bible app. "Here it is: In the day of prosperity, be joyful, but in the day of adversity, consider: God has made the one as well as the other, so that no one can discover anything that will come after him."

Rick whistles. "That'll preach on its own. What were you meditating on from it?"

"Well, it's humbling to remember that we don't have knowledge of the future or even the reasons we go through the things we do. I feel like this is my life right now, you know? I couldn't have predicted this pregnancy or living with Rarity! But knowing that God knew all of this and that he sends both hard and good times is a comfort to me."

"Amen. James says something similar about how we can't plan our lives, and that we should pursue God's will more than our plans."

"That's a word right there. What about you? Are you still in Luke?" He opens his mouth to answer, but the microwave goes off. "Hold that thought. Let me get our food." I grab the plate of four patties and place it on a mat on the breakfast bar, then I sit on a stool beside him.

"I'll pray for our food and then fill you in." I nod and close my eyes.

"Father, thank you for this food and the hands who prepared it. Bless both. In Jesus's name, amen."

"Amen," I eagerly reach for a patty. Usually, I have them weekly because they're served at church after the service ends. But since I'm no longer going there, I don't have them as frequently.

Rick inhales one of his patties and then talks. "I've finished Luke! I'm going to go more slowly later, but I wanted to get a feel for the book as a whole and its different themes."

"Nice. What are some things you're reflecting on?"

"I love how Luke highlights how loving Jesus is to those who would be on the margins of society or seen as lesser-than. Like, he mentions women I think more than any other gospel!"

"That's a good point to think about. Like, how are we, as a church, doing at being like Jesus in this way? Coming from a Jamaican church, I don't think we did inclusion well. Like, someone coming into the service who's not dressed up would be looked down upon, not pursued. Let's not even mention those with developmental specialties!" I shake my head in anger as I move on to my second patty.

"Facts. Even with the racial reckoning happening in the States and how mainstream evangelical churches are not reflecting the diversity of the kingdom. I've noticed online that whenever someone talks about growing in diversity, there's this quick rejection of the person because of critical race theory or not focusing on the gospel enough. But, like, loving the marginalized is being like Jesus!"

"Whoa, someone's getting heated."

Rick and I turn to see Rarity looking very amused and thoughtful.

"Yeah, I can get pretty passionate about this stuff." Rarity laughs.

"Well, clearly. What you were saying is interesting though, little bro. I don't know that I've ever heard Christians speak like that about race. I didn't know that Jesus was for the marginalized.

That's cool."

Rick and I exchange smiles. This is such a win. Hopefully, that'll stir some curiosity in her about Jesus.

"Earth to Ruthia, do you copy?" My mom's voice jolts me back to our conversation.

"Sorry about that."

"Thinking about your friend?" I can't help but laugh at the insinuation in her tone.

"He really is only my friend! He also just has amazing hazel eyes. So, I might have a crush? Is it possible to love someone and like someone else at the same time?"

"Yes. It is. How do you think people end up cheating on their spouses? It's not always that they've stopped loving them, you know, but that they let their hearts be open to someone else. Answer me this, do you think you would still have a crush on this guy if you were still dating your ex?"

I think about what she's just said. It makes sense, but it just feels like something I haven't heard talked about before. "Assuming that I would've still met Roderick, I would have found him physically attractive. But I don't think I would have a crush on him with my heart being so committed to my boyfriend."

She nods at my response. "That's what I thought. But now that you're no longer in a relationship with him, your heart's door is open. Maybe just a crack, but open just the same. My guess is that's where your crush is coming from."

"That makes sense. Thanks for that. It makes me feel less like an emotional ho."

She snorts at this. "You could never. Also, don't discount all the hormonal action taking place in your body right now. Sometimes, women can experience a higher sex drive, which can lead to you being holistically more horny-"

"Mom!" That word felt so incompatible with my mother. I'd never heard her say it before. She rolls her eyes at me.

"Please, Ruthia. I'm just giving you the science." The twinkle in her eyes shows me she just enjoys teasing me and I laugh. "So, anyway. You're not sure if you want to get with the baby's father, for a couple of reasons. No wonder the practicalities of it all feel so unknown to you. Parenting as a single mother is so different from doing so as part of a unit. What about financially? How are you feeling in that respect?"

"That, I'm not too worried about. You know that I just finished school -"

"And I'm so, so proud of you for that! I can't wait to go to my baby's graduation." The pride is clear in her voice.

"Thank you, Mom." We exchange warm smiles. "A daycare actually offered me a full-time job. I'm meeting with my future boss later today to go over the details of my start date and everything."

"That's wonderful! If you begin in June, you should accumulate enough hours for maternity leave with government compensation. And by I think, I mean I was on their website earlier this week reading up on all the requirements because I was freaking out about you having finances for the baby."

I raise my eyebrows in surprise. "Well, dang. Breathe, mom. God has got me covered, okay?"

"Trust me, that's what He's been telling me. He's been reminding me you're His daughter first, and that He is more than able to meet your needs. He's Your good shepherd: I'm just a momma sheep."

"A fabulous momma sheep."

"Thank you. And do you think you'll continue to live where you're staying right now?"

"I don't know. I haven't talked to my host about that yet."

"Well, maybe let's plan to do that in the next few days. It might help to ease some of the anxiety you're feeling. Remember, anxiety flourishes -"

"- in avoidance."

"That's right. How has your mental health been with everything? Specifically, how has the anxiety been?"

"So, after that night when Daddy kicked me out, it was pretty bad." She nods, her face sad. "But God has been showing me He, as you said before, is a good shepherd and worthy of my trust. And He's surrounded me with some kind people. I just wish he would give me some clarity on what to do with my romantic life. These mixed feelings are a menace."

"Well, that I can pray for."

"Thanks, Mom. I need it. How have things been at hom- at the house?" It feels strange that my mom's home isn't my home anymore.

"Well, your father and I aren't speaking." I gasp. I've never known that to happen in their marriage. "What he did was unacceptable, and he refuses to acknowledge that his response was wrong. I cannot be more gracious than God. And in His grace, He still requires us to agree with Him that we sinned and turn from it."

"Okay, Deaconess Walkins! You better preach!" She shakes her head, laughing. "For real though, Mom, that's facts. I never thought of it that way before, but you're right."

"Thank you. I know it's the right boundary, but it's a hard one. I love your father, but I can barely look at him without feeling angry about how he treated you. We should be spending time together on our couch in the living room, not at a Cinnabon in a mall. And he's to blame for that." She shakes her head again, this time sad. "I can't even sleep in the same bed as him. I've been staying in your room instead. Oh! That reminds me." She reaches below the table and pulls out a duffel bag. I didn't even notice that she'd had that with her when she arrived.

"I've packed some more things for you. I grabbed more of your shoes, your spring jacket and a few nicer things just in case you have somewhere special to go."

"Mom, you didn't have to do this! You'd already packed me so much before!"

"I'm your mom. I'm supposed to take care of you. And if this and prayer are the only ways I can do that in this season, then that's what I'm going to do."

"You're the best mom I could've ever asked for. I can only hope that I'll be like you."

"Oh Ruthie," she takes my hands. "Listen to me carefully." I nod and lean closer to her. She meets my eyes with hers, looking determined. "You'll be better than me." I shake my head. "Don't do that. I have always wanted my ceiling to be your floor. And sure, the way this started may not be ideal. But you are a capable, kind, and godly woman. You are going to be a phenomenal mother. Of that, I have no doubt."

I let her words wash over me. I let them sink in.

Capable.

Kind.

Godly.

Phenomenal.

Her words are a soothing aloe to the burns of my father's words to me that night. "Thank you, mommy," Like when we first embraced, she cups one side of my face with one of her hands. I lean into her. She feels like comfort, safety and home.

"Oh, my Ruthia Nicole Sapphire Walkins. May the Lord bless you and protect you; may the Lord make his face shine on you and be gracious to you; may the Lord look with favour on you and give you peace. Amen."

"Amen." I receive the blessing and the healing that it gives me. "Mommy, I'm so glad that we were able to meet today. I needed this. I needed you." I shake my head. "No, put that in the present tense. I need you."

"And I need you, Bella. What's a mother without a child? Could we maybe see about doing this weekly?"

"That would be great! I just need to figure out what my work schedule will be, and I'll let you know a time that works. Speaking of, I think I need to get going for that meeting with my boss."

"Do you need a ride?"

More time with my mom instead of on a bus? It's not even a question. "That would be helpful. Thank you."

"You're most welcome. Let's go."

We throw out our plates, and I follow her to where she parked. As much as so many things have changed, I'm glad that our relationship has only done so for the better.

Chapter 11

Roderick smiles at me from the couch in the living room as I walk through the door.

"Hey, Nin!"

His greeting cheers me as butterflies in me awaken. I try to tell them to go back to resting, to no avail.

"Hey, how has your day been?" I kick off my shoes.

"Not bad. I'm feeling restless though. It's weird to not have assignments to do." He responds as I plop down onto the other side of the couch and sigh. "How are you doing? Rough day?"

"Well, I just had my first OB appointment."

"That's a big deal!"

"Thank you, it is. But now I'm feeling overwhelmed."

"Ah. I know what this calls for; the perfect solution to your overwhelm and my restlessness."

"And that would be?"

"A surprise, if you're willing to indulge me a bit." I am about to shake my head, but then he says, "Do you trust me?"

I do more than I should. "Do I look like Jasmine to you?"

His laugh is loud in response. "I couldn't resist the most iconic line of my favorite Disney movie."

"Fair enough. True story though, growing up, I thought Jasmine and Pocahontas were Black. When Disney announced the Princess and the Frog, everyone was like, 'Yay! We finally have a Black Disney princess.' And I was so confused by what they meant." I laugh at myself, but his gaze is thoughtful.

"It's both cute and sad that little Nin had so little representation that she grabbed onto any princess of color she could."

His words open up the door to a self-awareness yet to be explored. "I never thought of it that way, but that's what I was doing! And the answer to your question is yes. I do trust you."

He smiles at me, lines around his eyes crinkling and it's hard to look away. I need to get a grip.

"Okay, let's go before you change your mind." He jumps up from the couch, then he offers me his hand.

I take it and the butterflies go nuts. It's so warm and somehow strong? It just makes me feel so safe.

As soon as I'm standing, I let go and head for my shoes.

"Do I need to change for this adventure?" I ask him, gesturing to my patterned maxi skirt and plain black tee.

"Hmm. You might want to change into jeans or something on the bottom."

"Gotcha, be right back!"

Before long, we're in his car and driving to our destination. We're in a more industrial part of the city.

"Should I regret my decision to trust you? This looks like the scene of a murder. Are you an axe murderer?"

"You're hot."

What? Did I hear him correctly? "Huh?"

"I meant your guess was hot, as in you're thinking in the right direction. Not that you're not hot. You know what? I'm just going to stop talking."

He's stammering, and it's adorable. I let the unintended compliment land on me before I put him out of his misery. "No worries, Rick. Breathe."

"Well, thanks. Here we are!" He turns into a parking spot and I see a sign that says 'Far Shot.'

"Where are we?"

"You'll see as soon as we get inside." We exit the car, and he holds the door to 'Far Shot' open for me.

I step into a large open space with different open wooden stalls and tables across from them lining the wall. I peek into one of the stalls and see targets on the back wall.

Before I ask Rick where we are, a South Asian guy walks up to him and gives him a bro hug. "Yo, need to burn off some energy, eh?"

"Guilty as charged. Max, this is Ruthia. Ruthia, Max. I think this is her first time doing axe throwing." He gestures to me, and I wave at his friend. Axe throwing? How cool!

"Yes, it will be my first time. But I'm excited."

"Sweet, well, Rod has been here enough times to show you the ropes. If you need any help, I'll be walking around. It'll be easy to find me. Let me go get your axes." I notice some girls in a stall doing archery.

"Can we do archery in addition to axe throwing?"

"Sure thing! I'll be back in a few minutes with everything you'll need." His response makes me clap my hands in glee. "You can head over to the last stall. It'll give you guys the most privacy." He adds, giving Rick a completely unsubtle wink.

"Bro, it's not even like that."

Max looks at me and then back at Rick. "Well, it should be."

I laugh at how forward Max is and walk toward the stalls, heading to the last one.

"Thanks for this! It's something I've always wanted to try but never gotten around to."

"I'm glad you're down for this! And don't worry, I checked to see if it was safe for pregnant women. And it completely is."

I'm shook by his thoughtfulness. My pregnant condition hadn't even occurred to me.

"Thanks for looking into that! How many times have you done this?"

"Hmm. This will be my 7th time, I think?"

"Wow. That's a lot. Although I shouldn't be surprised, considering that you're a military man." He chuckles at my teasing, shaking his head.

"I knew you would draw that connection." I am about to respond when Max shows up with axes, bows, and arrows in tow. He places them on a nearby table. "Here's everything you need. Have fun!"

Once he walks away, Rick turns toward me. "What do you want to start with?"

"Let's start with the axes."

"Okay, consider your request granted. Although before we start, maybe we should order some food? It's a bring-your-own food type of place and they let us have food delivered here, too."

I nod at his suggestion. "That's wise. I'm feeling for some good Jamaican food. Mind if we get that?"

"That sounds great." He takes out his phone. We order some jerk chicken, rice and peas and Caribbean soft drinks from one of my favorite places, Portland Jerk.

Once that's done, Rick takes off his sweater. He's in an army green t-shirt that is almost too small for him. And by that I mean, his muscular build fills out the shirt nicely.

Very nicely.

I look away and put my attention toward taking off my sweater as well.

He hands me an axe, and it's lighter than I expected. I say so and he nods.

"Yep, this is a specific axe for axe throwing. It's not one that chops wood, which is why it requires less force to throw it than you'd expect."

"Teach me, O wise one. I am your eager student."

"Well, young butterfly -"

"I'm pretty sure it's grasshopper, Rick." I butt in and he shakes his head to disagree with me.

"What happened to me being the teacher? You are more like a butterfly than a grasshopper to me, Nin; so that's what I'll call you." I feel my face warm and am very thankful for my dark skin that conceals my blushing.

"Now, back to your lesson. Let's head over to the target area, young butterfly." I follow him to the stall where there are two targets on the back wall, about 6 feet apart. He stops me at a line on the floor.

"Now, the recommended technique for pregnant

women is the two-handed throw. So you put two hands on the axe, holding it like a golf club." He demonstrates for me with his axe, and I try to mimic him.

"You're doing great. Now you're going to want to grip it lightly and bring it in front of your face, keeping the axe head parallel to the floor." I follow his lead.

"Now, you're going to want to lean back with your hands, bringing the axe over and behind your head and then bring it back to where it was initially to release it." I go through the motions of what he's saying. "That's it, Nin. I think you're ready to go."

I take a deep breath and then do what he showed me. The axe flies toward the wall and then bounces off of it, falling to the floor. Rick goes to pick it up for me and then comes back with the kindest eyes.

"Welp, I can only go up from here, right?"

He nods.

"Right. Now, the reason that happened was that you flicked your wrist when you released the axe. That's over-rotation. You want it to be one fluid motion when you throw. Is it okay if I help you practice that?"

I nod my head, confused. Isn't that what he's already doing? Then he moves behind me, and I feel his arms around my own, his hands on top of my hands on the axe. Good thing too, or I would've dropped it in shock. It takes all the self-restraint I have not to lean back into him. I take a breath to relax my body, and then I realize that he's tense as well.

Could our proximity be affecting him, too?

"Okay, so now we're going to bring the axe in

front of your face, now over and behind our heads and then bring it forward to release." He narrates our actions and when we release, the axe lands on the wall! Not near the center, but it's there.

"I did it!" Without thinking about it, I turn around and give him a hug. My head just reaches his shoulder and for a moment, I'm tempted to lean my head against him and just stay in his arms. They're warm and strong and make me feel safe. But I come to my senses and step out of the hug before it goes on for too long.

He clears his throat and gives me a warm smile. "Well done, young butterfly."

"Thank you, O wise teacher of mine. Now, as the youth say, show us your stuff!" He laughs and goes to pick his axe off of the floor. He goes behind the line that's lined up for his target and throws his axe with one hand. It lands just to the right of the center.

"You disappoint me. I was expecting a bullseye."

"Wow, so encouraging."

I giggle at his sarcasm.

"No excuses, military man, show me where my tax dollars are going!"

He laughs and goes to grab his axe from his target, then gets mine for me, too. Such a gentleman.

"Alright, civilian. Let me show you how I protect our country." He throws his axe with two hands this time and hits it right in the center.

I clap for him, and he bows dramatically. "You're welcome."

Then we hear a phone buzz from the table. We both go to see which one it is, and it's his. Our delivery guy is here. "I'll go meet the guy," he says and heads to the front. While he's gone, I try another throw by myself and feel proud when it lands on the wall - and even closer to the center than before! I jump and squeal.

"Okay, go off, Nin!" I turn to see Rick holding a plastic bag with brown paper bags and two drinks inside of it.

"It's the improvement for me."

He laughs, putting the food down on the table where our sweaters are.

"Do you want to stop to eat or keep on going?"

"I'm not too hungry yet. I'm down to keep throwing."

"Sweet. Same." And off we go.

Sometimes throwing at the same time, sometimes one after the other; teasing and encouraging each other along the way. It's so much fun and the stress release that I needed.

When my arm feels sore, I suggest we take a break to eat, and he agrees. After a quick prayer, we tuck into the meal.

"So, I've been curious. Why the military?"

"So, tell me more about your day?"

Our words get jumbled together since we spoke at the same time.

"It's okay, I can answer first." He might be the most agreeable guy I've ever met.

"Well, growing up, whenever it was Remembrance Day, I would always get so choked up. It would lowkey be embarrassing." I try to picture a younger Roderick trying to hide his tears at a school assembly; it's an adorable image.

"And my favorite movies would always be war

ones. Just seeing people being willing to risk their lives for others has always moved me. It felt like an easy decision to join the Canadian Armed Forces. And there are all these different roles I could play! It's not just guys with guns fighting terrorists. The army is like its own small community with its own doctors, musicians, you name it." His evident joy in sharing this with me is everything.

"It's just a bonus that they also will pay for my education. So, I decided I wanted to be a therapist in the army and just finished my undergrad in psych from Queen's. However, since coming to faith, I've been interested in chaplaincy. I don't just want to care for people's mental health, but their spiritual health, too. I figure it's a way for me to meet and encourage fellow Christians who serve and have opportunities to journey with people who don't know Jesus. I'm thinking about doing a Master's degree in spiritual care. The application is due next week."

I look at him, stunned at what he's shared. "That's amazing! Like, really. I love all of this for you! It's clear to me that this is where God has called you, and I love that you get to serve both God and our country in this calling. I will totally pray for you during your application process. I'm sure you'll get in."

"I really appreciate that, Ruthia. Thank you."

His voice is quiet now, bashful. I want to take his hand and give it an encouraging squeeze, but I refrain. Would that be a weird thing for a friend to do for another friend? And besides, would I want to let go?

"Alrighty, my turn then. So, the appointment was good. Dr. Parks is as kind as Rare said she was, and it's such a privilege to have a Black female doctor. There's so few of them." I shake my head at that.

"It started off pretty chill, like a normal checkup with my family doctor. You know, blood pressure, stethoscope, getting my height and weight. And then I got to hear my baby's heartbeat, which was wonderful."

"That must be a beautiful experience."

I smile at the awe in his voice.

I nod. "It is! But then it kind of went downhill from there. We had to go over my medical history, and my family's medical history, and then she asked about the baby's father's medical history. And I realized I know next to nothing about it! And there are so many tests that need to be done for this pregnancy to screen for any problems. I never realized how many ways pregnancy can go wrong. Now, I'm left feeling anxious about whether this pregnancy will be healthy, and I need to get answers to the questions she asked from Shane. That's why I wasn't in the best mood when I got home."

"That makes complete sense. How are things between you two?" His voice is tentative as he asks this question. "But you don't have to answer that if you don't want to. No pressure."

"Chill, I'm willing to talk about it. I don't know how to answer, though. He's been pretty diligent about texting me daily with words of affirmation. And yesterday, I got another video with him praying for me and the baby. It's just that I don't know what to do about our relationship, or lack thereof. I don't know if I want to be with him or if I should just be with him for the baby's sake. Truthfully, I avoid thinking about it when I can. And I haven't been praying about it either." I didn't expect to say all of that. "Sorry, that was a lot -"

"No need to apologize, Nin. I asked, and I wanted an honest answer. How else am I going to know how to pray for you?" He gives me an amiable smile.

"Well, thanks for listening. I only have Gaelle to talk to about these things."

"What about friends from school or church?"

"I don't have friends at my church. Being the pastor's daughter makes you kind of a social pariah. I have plenty of acquaintances, but no friends. And then at school, there are girls in my program that I'm close to, but they're not believers. They also all love Shane. I'm pretty sure I won't get an unbiased response from them." I shrug. "There are a few friends from the Christian club on campus. I've never really gotten to know them deeply, though. Mostly because I was so focused on my relationship with Shane, I guess." It dawns on me how much of my life revolved around my relationship with him.

"Well, I'm thankful to know you, Ruthia. I count it a privilege to be someone who can be with you as part of this process." His voice is so sincere, his eyes so warm. I feel my eyes getting ready to shed tears and force them back.

"Thanks, Roderick. I'm all done with my food now. Are you good to go back?"

"Bet. Let's do some archery this time."

"Get ready to be the student now, Rick." I tease as I get up to throw away the food's packaging.

"Okay, you're finna get your Katniss Everdeen on then?"

I laugh. "Well, before there was Katniss, there was Susan from Narnia and she was who I wanted to be when I was a kid." I pick up a bow and the container for the arrows; slinging the sack over my shoulder.

"Say less. Let's shoot some arrows."

"Yes, let's." And we do.

I've heard it said that the way one heals from trauma is through play, and that makes sense to me. There's something about being safe enough to let your guard down and laugh and be silly without fear of rejection. It's a perfect way to start my weekend and throw my heart into a tailspin because I like this guy. And it's more than just gorgeous eyes.

Lord, help me.

Chapter 12

I keep rewatching the end of this week's video as I lay on my bed.

"Amen." He finishes his prayer and then looks straight into the camera. His dark eyes pierce my soul.

"Thia, if you're willing, I would love to talk to you. I miss your voice. I'm free all day today. You can call at any time. If you don't feel ready, I'll understand. But you miss a hundred percent of the shots you don't take. So, I'm shooting my shot, and we'll see how it lands. Love you. Hopefully, talk to you soon!"

Do I want to talk to him? It's been weird not interacting with him. It's been a month since our breakup and three weeks of him trying to get us back together. Three weeks of these short but wonderful messages of his love for me. I scroll up to re-read them.

Shane Reid
7:16 am
You love Jesus more than you love me

Shane Reid

7:16 am
Your love for children. It's amazing how kind and caring you are to them; I look forward to seeing you   be   a   mom.

Shane Reid
7:16 am
You have a servant's heart; whether it's in prayer or caring for friends who are hurting, you display a Christ-like attitude seeking to serve rather than be served.

Shane Reid
7:16 am
You are easy to rest with; whether it's watching a movie with you or spending time with Jesus in the same place as you, being with you is always a blessing

Shane Reid
7:16 am
I love learning about you; how your mind works and how you see the world; you think in ways that I don't and show me how the gospel connects to little and big things in life.

Shane Reid
7:16 am
You have an incredible memory

Shane Reid
7:16 am
You love to read; your love for books has helped

me grow in my love for reading

Shane Reid
7:16 am
You treasure my things; there are sweaters, t-shirts and hats that I loved but loved seeing you in so much more

Shane Reid
7:16 am
You confront your sin and are quick to confess and repent; you inspire me to live a more holy life

Shane Reid
7:16 am
You have an eclectic and classy fashion style. I look forward to the outfits you choose and how you'll put things together

Shane Reid
7:16 am
You're gorgeous; I think you know from our history how attracted I am to you.

Shane Reid
7:16 am
You literally can't function without spending time with God in his word

Shane Reid
7:16 am
You show kindness in your everyday interactions, a simple "thank you" to a bus driver being one

example.

Shane Reid
7:16 am
Your eyes and how they are always so full of love for me

Shane Reid
7:16 am
You're hilarious and always trying to make me laugh

Shane Reid
7:16 am
You remind me of the gospel when I'm discouraged and hopeless

Shane Reid
7:16 am
You're a black woman; not only have I learned more about the challenges of being a black woman, but I can share my struggles as a black man with you and know that you understand me

Shane Reid
7:16 am
Your smile always displays joy in the Lord, and I never grow tired of seeing it

Shane Reid
7:16 am
You're ticklish and a tickle monster at heart. This makes me so happy, and I look forward to the day

when it is appropriate.

Shane Reid
7:16 am
The fragility you show gives me the courage to reveal my own vulnerabilities.

Shane Reid
7:16 am
Your trust in the man God is shaping me into has increased my confidence in the work God is doing in my life.

Sigh. He has been faithful to what he said he'd do.

"Lord, what should I do? Please, give me wisdom." I pray and then quiet myself, my thoughts, and my voice. And just wait.

A few minutes go by and then a verse comes to mind.

"Instead, be kind to one another, tender-hearted, graciously forgiving each other, just as God in Christ also has graciously forgiven you."

Have I forgiven him? Have I released the anger I feel at him hurting me?

Yes, I have. I'm no longer angry, now I just miss him. I miss what we had. Not having him in my day-to-day life is like losing a limb. I feel this phantom pain, like a part of me should be present but isn't.

Sigh. Let's call him and see what happens. I swipe through my phone to his contact information and then call him.

He answers it before the first ring finishes.

"Ruthia? You called. Thank you for calling." He sounds surprised, relieved and grateful. His live voice relaxes me. Its familiarity is comforting.

"Hi, Shane."

He sighs contentedly. "You do not know how great it is to hear your voice."

"Was there something in particular you wanted to talk about?"

"Honestly? I just missed you and I guess I wanted to get a read on how you're feeling toward me? But, no pressure. You don't have to share anything if you don't want to."

"Well, I've forgiven you. I don't remember when it happened, but it is true. I'm not angry with you anymore. And I haven't stopped loving you either. But, I just can't understand what made you switch on me. Why did you do it?" I didn't realize that this question had been bothering me so much. But it had been.

He takes his time replying, "That's a valid question, and I hope you'll let me use computer terms to answer?"

I nod and then remember that he can't see me. "Permission granted."

"I got scared of the future and how it would change and it's like my system stopped working, like a website or app crashing. I just needed to reboot somehow, and it felt like the easiest way to do so was to stage a reset, and that looked like walking away from you. It was a self-preservation instinct. It was my selfish flesh. I should have never walked away from you and our baby. I should have stayed and prayed with you for our future. Leaving you is the biggest regret of my life."

He's saying everything I want to hear, but it's not enough. I cry at how messed up everything is and how confused I feel. I've forgiven him and I love him, but something's still missing.

"Crap. Ruthia, are you crying? I'm sorry for making you cry. I've been the source of way too many tears for you. I'm so sorry." Now he sounds choked up too.

"Thank you for everything you've said. I get you were scared and trying to protect yourself. I was also scared. And you left me alone. You have no idea what I've gone through because of that; how it feels to be abandoned at your literal lowest point."

"You're right. I don't know how that feels. But I want you to know that I won't abandon you again. I-"

"But how can I know that for sure? How can I know that the next time something hard comes, you won't leave me again, leave us again? Because it's going to be hard, Shane. We're going to face challenges, and I need to know that you'll stay through them. I need to trust -" I stop speaking. That's what's missing, trust. There is love and forgiveness, but no trust.

"Ruthia? Did the phone cut out?"

"I'm still here. Something just occurred to me. I know you love me, and I love you, Shane. And I even forgive you, but I don't trust you. And I don't know how to trust you again."

"That makes sense." His voice sounds defeated. "I'll do anything to earn your trust, Ruthia. But in the meantime, would you be willing to trust God in me? Because I have the Holy Spirit and I love God, I can be someone who is trustworthy. Do you think that's possible?"

I think about his question. It feels like he's asking a lot out of me. It'll take the Holy Spirit in me to give him this chance. But if I trust the Spirit's power in my life, I can trust Him in anyone's. Even Shane.

"It's possible, Shane. But I need to know. What do you want? Let's say you earn my trust back. What's next?"

"I want to marry you, Ruthia."

I gasp, and my heart feels like it could burst. "Shane, those are big words."

"And I mean them. My goal is not to date you, it's to marry you and be a family. To parent this child in the Lord, not as co-parents but married parents." He sounds so sure, and I'm stumped. My heart is beating wildly. I can't tell if it's from anxiety or excitement or some mashup of both.

"I don't know what to say to that."

"You don't have to have a response right now, okay? Just give me a chance to show that I'm a guy whose proposal you can accept. Can you do that?" My heart calms down. This, this makes sense. This I can do.

"Yes, I can." I hear a sigh of relief.

"Praise God. I don't know if I could've handled you saying no."

I laugh, and it releases all the nervous energy I was holding onto. He laughs too, and it's nice to laugh with him.

"So, what app are you using to track the pregnancy? You've been right on the money with all the milestones."

"What to Expect. There's even a forum for dads which has been really enlightening. How are you doing, health-wise? Are you and the baby okay? I pray for you every night and that you won't have a miscarriage." My heart melts. He sounds so concerned.

"I've thrown up a handful of times, but otherwise I'm good; just exhausted all the time. That's supposed to get better in a few weeks. As far as I know, the baby has been doing well. I had my first appointment last week and got to hear the baby's heartbeat."

"Wow."

"I know. Everything looked good on the ultrasound as well. I took a picture of the picture that they gave me. Would you like me to send it to you?"

He takes no time to answer. "Yes!"

I chuckle to myself at his excitement. "Alrighty, I'll send it to you once this call ends."

"Thanks, Ruthia." I can hear the smile in his voice.

"Hey, can you let me know if there are any diseases that run in your family? Cancer, cardiovascular, diabetes, etc? I just remembered that I need this information for my doctor."

"Yes, to diabetes, no cancer or heart problems. I think I have a cousin with sickle cell, but that's it. I can ask my parents, though."

"Do your parents know about this situation?"

"Yes, I told them the same day you told me."

"And how did they react?"

"They were shocked and disappointed, then they got excited. Have you told yours yet?" His voice is cautious, and I appreciate that. I don't want to get into all of what happened, though. I don't trust him enough for that yet.

"I have, but I actually need to get going." I hate lying, but I don't know how else to avoid his question.

"Okay, I'm humbled to have even had a little of your time, Thia. Have a great rest of your Thursday. I love you."

"Thanks, Shane." I pause for a moment and then decide to go for it. "I love you too." And then I hang up.

I stare at the ceiling and sigh. Apparently, loud enough for Rarity to hear me from the hallway. "Thia? You okay in there?"

"Define okay." She laughs and opens the door. "Are you good with me coming in?"

I nod, and she does, lying next to me on the bed.

"So, what's the sigh about?" She wastes no time.

"Shane."

"Ah, the ex. What about him?"

"Well, the ex wants to become the husband."

She gasps.

"That's exactly how I responded!" I sigh again.

"The audacity! He's lucky if you even forgive him, much less get back together or marry him!" She sat up, resting against the bed's headrest, verifiably enraged on my behalf.

"Well, Rare, I've already forgiven him. That's not the problem here."

"You what?!" She leans over and looks at my face. "You're serious."

I choose my words carefully. "Yes, I am. God commands us to forgive people who have hurt us. It's not a matter of if, but when. Forgiveness isn't optional."

"Hmph. But why do you have to forgive? Like, why would God command that?" Her confusion is genuine.

"Well, Jesus tells this story of three guys: let's call them Guy A, Guy B and Guy C. Guy B owes Guy A a crap ton of money, but Guy A releases him from the debt."

"Nice guy." Rarity comments.

"Right? Now, Guy C owes Guy B a much smaller amount of money, but Guy B bankrupts him and sends him to prison."

"What a hypocrite!"

"I know! But Jesus told that story to teach a lesson about forgiveness. We're like guy B. We have wronged God so much. But, God forgives us. If we choose not to forgive those who hurt us, we're acting like guy B in the story. We would then become hypocrites. That's why we have to forgive, because we've been forgiven." I hope that this isn't too preachy, and that this doesn't scare her away from spiritual conversations.

She's silent for a while and when she speaks, I barely hear her. "I don't think I could forgive my ex like that. It just feels impossible to do so."

"Facts. I totally relate."

"But you have forgiven Shane. I can see it on your face and in your demeanor." She points out.

"Yep, but I had help in doing so. Forgiveness, like a lot of things Jesus told us to do, doesn't come naturally to us. That's why we need supernatural help, and God gives us that in the power of the Holy Spirit."

"Interesting. What is the Holy Spirit? I feel like

the only thing I know about the Holy Spirit is that people said it was the reason that people would get all weird at church.”

“Yep. Some of that is legit, but a lot of it is foolishness.”

She laughs. “It’s the candor for me.”

I laugh with her. “Put simply, the Holy Spirit is God’s personal presence living inside of Christians. He helps us do the things that we couldn’t do on our own, amongst other things.”

“That makes sense. So, God just expects you to forgive and forget?”

I roll my eyes. “No, that saying isn’t even in the Bible. He expects us to forgive, but he doesn’t command us to trust or to be in relationships with people with no boundaries. Like, I know I love Shane, and I’ve forgiven him, but I don’t trust him anymore.”

“Super valid. So, what are you going to do?”

I sigh again, and she laughs. “Enough sighing!”

“Well, I have no clue what I’m going to do. Shane needs to prove himself somehow.” I shrug.

“I guess he’ll need the Holy Spirit for that, since it seems pretty impossible to me.”

“Awesome application of what we were just talking about.” I hold up my hand for a high five, and she returns it.

“Well, you know, I’m not just a pretty face.”

“Noted. Someone’s feeling herself.”

“Well, self-love is something that I’m trying to grow in.” I’m touched by her vulnerability.

“Facts. I feel like I need to grow in that as well. It’s enough to make a girl ...” and then I sigh again.

She laughs and gets off the bed.

"That's my cue to leave. I've gotta wake up Cynthia. I let her sleep in this morning. See you later."

I wave goodbye. Jeeze, it's been a full morning.

Chapter 13

I don't function well without having things to do. This interim time of finishing my program and starting work with Michelle is supposed to be restful. Instead, it's frustrating. I have a countdown on my phone for my start date, June 12. The next 25 days cannot go fast enough. Even with the books that Shane has been sending me, I'm still bored. I can't believe it, but I have even reached my limit on reading.

Frustrated, I pick up my phone and look over my checklist of things to do for this pregnancy. Bingo! I know it's early with me only being 12 weeks along, but I can at least work on my registry for baby stuff.

I go to the Amazon app on my phone and start a registry. It's super easy. They even have different categories and a checklist to make sure you hit all the essentials.

As I scroll through the checklist, I see more and more things that I've never thought of. I feel a pain in my chest and try to take deep breaths.

Breathe, Ruthia, breathe. Let's just start with the first category, baby steps - no pun intended.

I tap on the first category, strollers and car seats, but it only amplifies my anxiety as I see the prices. I didn't realize that strollers are so expensive. And there are so many options. Do I want a jogging stroller? Do I want a stroller that connects to a car seat? I don't even have a car to put a car seat in!

My breaths become more and more shallow and the pain in my chest is overwhelming. My mind races.

I can't breathe. I can't breathe. I can't breathe. I'm such a wimp. How am I supposed to be a mother? I can't even choose a freaking stroller, and I'm supposed to take care of a whole human? I can't do this. I can't do this. It's all going to go wrong. I'm going to ruin this kid's life just by being their mother. And oh no, what if they inherit my anxiety? It's all going to be terrible. There's nothing good ahead. The future looks doomed. Doomed. Doomed.

I curl into a ball in one of the couch corners, my knees up to my face and my arms around my legs. I just want to protect myself. I want to feel safe. But I'm not being attacked by an outside force. The assault is from my mind. I can't protect myself. I'll never be safe.

I sob.

I'm not safe. I can't do this. My future is doomed.

I'm not safe. I can't do this. My future is doomed.

I'm not safe. I can't do this. My future is doomed.

These words are on a loop in my mind, and then I hear my name.

"Ruthia?" The voice is worried. Is this voice real or is this my mind playing tricks on me? I hear quick footsteps and then the voice again.

"Ruthia?"

All I can do is cry. This voice is so kind, but it's not real. My thoughts are my only reality.

"Ruthia, it's Roderick. I'm here. You're not alone."

I blink my eyes open to see a blurry Rick. He's on his knees on the floor in front of the couch, in front of me.

"I ... can't ... breathe." My words come out in wheezes since my breathing is so shallow.

He nods as if he understands what I'm saying. "You're having a panic attack?" I nod.

"Okay, let's get you breathing." He sits beside me on the couch and gently takes one of my hands. Then he puts it on the left side of his chest, over his heart. I feel the steady thrum of his heartbeat and his chest moving up and down.

"Try to match me, Nin. Deep breaths in ... deep breaths out." He says slowly, in sync with his own deep breaths.

I try, but all I can do is shake. The thoughts are still screaming at me. I can't focus. I want to tell him this, but all that comes out are the thoughts.

"I'm not safe. I can't do this. My future is doomed. I'm not safe. I can't do this. My future is doomed. I'm not safe. I can't do this. My future is doomed." I'm hysterical, maniacally repeating those words over and over again.

I pull my hand away to cover my face, but Rick clasps it in place.

"You're a fighter, Nin. You can do this. All you need to do is focus on the thumps of my heart."

I put all my energy into focusing on my hand and the beats it's feeling. And then the thoughts recede, and my breaths become less shallow.

"Nin, look at me."

I shake my head, now mortified at having an attack in front of Rick.

"Please." It's the pleading tone of his voice that gets me to look up. His eyes are hazel pools of compassion. I'm stunned and can't look away.

"Nin, you are safe. You can do all things through Christ. And your future is good." His words feel like a cool breeze on a scorching day.

"Say it with me, Nin. I am safe."

"I am safe."

"Louder, Nin. I can do all things through Christ."

"I can do all things through Christ."

"Now, let's yell out this last one. My future is good!"

I take a deep breath and shout at the top of my lungs. "MY FUTURE IS GOOD!"

I smile. Man, that felt good.

"Thanks, Rick." Those words feel inadequate to describe my gratitude, but it's all I've got.

"You're welcome." He smiles at me, and it feels like the butterflies in my stomach have just sighed. Like they can rest now because they know that we're safe.

"Can I ask what happened? Or would that trigger another attack?"

"I got super overwhelmed with the baby registry." I try to shrug it off.

"Hey, I remember when Rare was making hers. It's pretty stressful. Your feelings are valid, Nin. I know sometimes anxiety comes because of uncertainty and feeling out of control. What's something that you can do right now that would make you feel more in control?"

I think about his question. And then it comes to me.

"My hair! It's been a long time since I've put in my extensions." And this is true. The fresh growth is super obvious and my braids have been looking a little ratty.

"Sweet! Let me go get us a pair of scissors and a plastic bag." He gets off the couch.

"Us?"

"Sorry, I presumed. I'm happy to help you take out your braids. I used to do it for my mom. But if you want to do this solo and have some 'me time', I will understand." He backtracks.

I'm touched by his offer and how considerate he's been to me. "I'm good for you to help me, Rick. Thanks for volunteering."

"Great, well sit on the floor at the foot of the couch and I can sit on the couch behind you."

Bemused, I follow his instructions and he's back soon with the bag and scissors. He positions himself so that I'm sitting square in between his legs.

"Do you want to watch a movie while we do this?" It takes all of my self-control not to lean into his touch.

"Personally, I'm not really in a movie mood. How about some music? We can go back and forth in song choices."

"That works for me."

"Cool, now from what I see, your hair ends here." I feel him point to a specific spot on one of my braids. "Are you good if I cut about an inch below this spot?"

"You really know what you're doing. It's the expertise for me. Yep, you can do that." He cuts off chunks of hair until there are a bunch of extensions on the floor. I put them into the plastic bag.

"I think I got all of them."

"Let the true work now begin. Well, let's give you the first choice. What song would you like?"

"Freedom is Dead by Demon Hunter." He says, after thinking for a moment.

I find it easily on YouTube and turn up the volume before hitting play.

I hear someone's guttural shouting and press stop.

"Oops, sorry. Maybe I clicked the wrong song?" I'm about to go look for another video. "No, that's the right one."

I turn around, making him drop the braid he was undoing, and look up at him with an eyebrow raised.

"That was music, then?"

He laughs, "Yes. I love heavy metal or screamo, as some people call it."

"So, this is unexpected. Clearly, it's your Caucasian half coming out." He laughs again.

"It's actually a superb song, Nin. It's about the dangers of cancel culture."

I shake my head as I turn back around. I guess everyone has to have a fatal flaw.

For his sake, I sit through the song and try my best to hear and understand the lyrics - to no avail.

"So, what do you think?"

I pause. "Erm. It's not my style of music." I can feel his hands in my hair, shaking from his laughter.

"Thanks for enduring it for me. I look forward to your song choice."

It's an easy pick: Armies by KB. My favorite song by my favorite artist. I rap along with him as I work through another braid. When it finishes, Rick takes his hands out of my hair and claps.

"Okay, so you're into rap - and not too shabby at it, either."

"You sound surprised,"

"I am. I pegged you for more indie pop."

"I enjoy music from almost every genre, except-"

"Screamo." We laugh together.

The rest of the afternoon passes by quickly as we work on my hair and share our favorite songs with each other. When the last braid is undone, I shake my head, enjoying how light it is. I turn around to face Rick and hold up my hand for a high-five. He returns it.

"Thanks for this, really. It would've taken a lot longer without your help. Teamwork does make the dream work."

"No worries. What are your plans for the rest of the day?"

I think again about my boredom from earlier. "Nothing. Why?"

"Well, I was going to put on a curry for dinner tonight. Once I have it on the stove, would you be down for some bootleg karaoke?"

I laugh. "What is bootleg karaoke?"

"Doing karaoke, but with YouTube videos instead of having a karaoke system."

This sounds fun. "Yeah, I'm down."

"Sweet. I should be ready in about 20 minutes."

"Works for me. I need to wash my hair, anyway."

I head to my bathroom and grab my Creme of

Nature Argan Oil shampoo and conditioner. Washing my hair feels so lovely. Once I'm done shampooing, I add in the conditioner and then put on a shower cap. I'll let this sit on my hair for a while. It needs some love.

I glance in the mirror as I get dressed. Gosh, I look downright wacky in this shower cap. What will Roderick think?

Wait, why do I care what he thinks? He's already seen me in a panic attack. I threw out embarrassment a few hours ago! I shake my head at my yo-yo-ing emotions.

When I leave my room, I smell curry. So much yum.

I poke my head into the kitchen to see Rick washing up a few dishes. "This smells great!" I walk over to where he is at the sink and dry the just-rinsed dishes. I was worried about my shower cap for no reason. He does not even notice it.

"Thanks, beef curry is one of my go-to meals."

I chuckle a bit. "You mean curry beef?"

"I said what I said." His tone is serious, but his raised eyebrows reveal that he's being playful.

"You're so Trini. Curry goes before the meat, not after."

He laughs at my correction. "Brave move, Nin, provoking the man who's making the food."

I hold up my hand in surrender. "Fine, fine, call it whatever you want as long as it tastes good."

He smiles at his small victory. "It should. I'll just let it simmer on the stove for a bit. You ready to get your karaoke on?"

"Bet." We head to the living room.

Once YouTube is up on the screen, we get going and it's a blast. Rick does a fantastically awful rendition of Man's Not Hot and I'm laughing so hard that my face hurts. Often, when we chat, we're serious. And that's great! But it's nice to just be goofy with each other.

When Rarity and Cynthia get home, I'm belting out the chorus to "I'll Make a Man Out of You" from Mulan while Rick cheers me on.

"Looks like you two have been having fun!"

Rick waits until I finish my performance before answering Rare. "We have been!"

"More Disney songs!" Cynthia's excitement is beyond endearing. "Hmm. What's a boy and girl song? What about the one with the flying carpet?"

"You're talking about the one from Aladdin, right?" She nods at my clarification.

"Yes! That's the one. Mommy Ruthia and Uncle Rod can do it!"

Rick and I exchange glances like we're asking each other whether we should do this. He shrugs and I nod. Then he turns to Cynthia, "As you wish, princess!"

Then we sing. And as we do, the lyrics hit me. A raw honesty permeates the song's vulnerable melody.

And I wonder, especially after everything that's happened this afternoon, whether there's a new world that I could explore too.

Chapter 14

It's time to talk to Rarity. I've been putting it off for the past month, ever since I last met with my mom, but I can't do it any longer. Plus, now is the perfect time since Rick has taken Thia out for an uncle-niece date. I find her sitting on a loveseat in her burgeoning library, reading a book.

"Rare. Is it okay if we chat for a few minutes?"

"Sure, Thia. What's up?"

I sit beside her and take a deep breath. "Hey, so thank you so much for your hospitality. It's been 6 weeks of me living here, but we never talked about the practical things. Like how long I can stay here, for instance. I also feel like I've just been mooching off of you, not paying rent or contributing to groceries."

She looks stunned. "Ruthia, you are an unemployed pregnant woman without a place to stay. I don't feel taken advantage of." She puts a hand on my knee. "I have more than enough funds and space and I want to use them to care for you. You've become family to me, like the little sister I always wanted - don't tell Roderick that. You can stay here for as long as you need; for the rest of your pregnancy and even postpartum. This is your home.”

I cry as she speaks, and she opens up her arms to me. I lean into her, “Thank you, Rarity. You are a gift from God.”

“Thanks, love. Now, I don’t want to hear about this again. I know you’re starting work soon, but I want you to focus on saving money and putting things toward the baby. We have groceries, rent, and so on covered. Understand?”

“Yes, ma’am.”

“Jeeze, wait to make me feel like an old woman, Ruthia!” I laugh with her. “Do you want to join me in reading?”

“Thanks for offering, but I’m going to go to my room and do my hair. It’s had a week to breathe, but now it’s time to put in some new braids.”

“I didn’t realize that you did it yourself! That’s impressive.”

“YouTube is one of the best teachers I’ve ever had. Have a good rest of your evening, Rare.”

I head to my room and as I’m cutting open the package of hair for my braids, my phone vibrates. I glance down to see that it’s Shane.

That’s weird. This is beyond his normal morning text.

Shane Reid
7:57 pm
Just texting to say that I miss our weekly movie nights. Watching movies alone sucks compared to watching them with you. Love you, bye!

I smile at his message. Rarity and Rick are great,

but the last time I watched a movie with them, they wanted it to be quiet the whole time. I thought I was going to burst with all my unsaid commentary. Before I can overthink it, I respond to his text.

Me   7:58 pm

I feel the same way. What was the next movie on our list, again?

Shane Reid
7:59 pm
I just checked it. We were supposed to watch the live filming of Hamilton.

I'm about to reply when I see the three dots that show that he is writing a message, so I decide to wait.

Shane Reid
7:59 pm
Would you be down to watch it with me tonight? It doesn't have to be in person, we can do GroupWatch on Disney Plus.

Well, I needed something to do while putting in my extensions, anyway. Why not?

Me   8:00 pm

Sounds like a plan!

Shane Reid
8:00 pm
Great, would you be down to do a phone call

while we watch? I want to hear your commentary.

My smile grows. He knows me so well.

Me   8:01 pm

Sure.

Shane Reid
8:01 pm
Sweet. Let me drop the link in your email.
Sent.

I rise from the bed, retrieve my laptop from my dresser, and check that the charger is plugged in. Then I pull up my email and see his message. I click on the link.

Me   8:04 pm

I'm in.

My phone buzzes as he calls me. Crap, why did I agree to do a phone call? Now I'm nervous! I take a deep breath to steady my nerves and then answer.

"Hello?"

"Hey, Thia." His voice is deep and warm and calms my body down. My heart may be all over the place, but my body isn't. It still associates Shane with safety.

"Hey, Shane. It's nice to hear your voice, live I mean."

"Same, Thia. You ready to start?"

"Yep, go for it!"

It opens with a Black guy doing a combo of singing and rapping. I'm captivated, and the music is lit.

"I love it already."

Shane laughs at my immediate reaction.

"This is a pretty lit start."

I bop to the music as I part my hair. This is going to be great.

We keep watching, exchanging thoughts as we do.

"I love his squad!" Shane comments.

"Burr is slick."

"Okay, these are my sisters. Women should be included in the sequel!"

"Facts."

"The way they portrayed the king is wild. His song is hilariously toxic."

"Oh, my goodness! The rewinding! They're even doing the choreography backwards!"

"She loves her sister's man. That's tough. Gaelle could never!"

"Oh, my goodness. Burr is low-key misunderstood. He seems passive, but he's just patient. His song may be my favorite thus far."

"She's pregnant! Ahh! Literally, she's my sister!"

"Okay, Hercules Mulligan! That's my boy!"

"The way they've interspersed all these different genres. Thomas's song is giving jazz."

"Ooooh. This rap battle slaps."

"Mans is basically emotionally cheating on his wife with his sister. They're wrong for those letters."

"Hamilton! Say no! Say no! Run like Joseph, bro!"

"Burr gets the best songs."

"Okay, I love George Washington. You better rest under your fig tree."

"Aww, Eliza. I feel you, sister. I know what it's like to be hurt and want to just eff it all." This story is starting to hit a little too close to home.

"Thia, I'm so sorry."

"I know. Let's just keep watching."

"No! His son dies! What the heck? Eliza can't take much more than this. I can't even imagine going through that."

"He's singing her melody! I can't even." I'm crying now.

"Do you want us to pause the movie?"

"No, let's keep going."

"So, that's why he kills him. Such a shame that he realized that they both could've flourished without harming the other."

"Wow. Eliza is the MVP."

The movie ends.

"That was incredible. We hopped on this way too late." Shane says.

"For real, we were sleeping on this. I'm going to be obsessively listening to this soundtrack for a while." I have about 7 braids left, maybe even less than that. Doing it has taken longer than normal because I was so engrossed in the play.

"Facts. What are some takeaways you have from it?"

I smile at him, asking our standard processing question.

"Well, even though the play is about Hamilton, it's Burr who I can't stop thinking about. His insecurity prevented him from being a man of integrity."

"Okay. You better preach on that, Thia!"

I laugh at him fooling around.

"But seriously, if he had been secure in his beliefs and values, he would have had the courage to make big moves. Also, he wouldn't have felt the need to kill Hamilton. It makes me think of insecurities in my life and their consequences."

"Hmm. I'll be praying that the Holy Spirit gives you that awareness."

I can hear the sincerity in his voice. He's not just saying it to be nice, he means it.

"What stood out for you?"

"There are so many things!" His enthusiasm makes me chuckle. "I feel like I may need a rewatch. The major thing for me, though, relates to Hamilton. He is an example of how one sinful decision can change the trajectory of your life. Like, his cheating on Eliza snowballed into financial shadiness, marital breakdown, political ruin, and the death of his son!"

"You're not wrong."

"Honestly, it made me think about us. How my stupid and selfish decision has affected us. Now I've 'forfeited my place in your heart', as Eliza said." His voice is serious and sad.

My instinct is to want to comfort him. "Hey, Shane. You still have a place in my heart."

"Really?" He sounds like he doesn't believe me.

"Really. Otherwise, tonight wouldn't have happened."

"That's fair. If I'm still in your heart... I have to ask where you're at regarding us getting back together?"

I sigh. "Honestly? Tonight reminded me that you weren't just my boyfriend, you were one of my best friends. And it felt easy being with you for the past few hours. Like things were back to normal."

"This all sounds great, yet I feel like there's a 'but' coming." He sounds tentative.

"There is, but I still don't trust you. And I can't put into words how you would go about earning it."

"Thanks for being so transparent with me. I appreciate it." I finish the last braid. That's my cue to wrap things up and go to bed.

"Hey, Shane, I have to get going."

"Okay. Thank you for tonight. I hope you have a restful sleep. Night, Thia, I love you."

He hangs up the phone right after, so he doesn't hear me whisper, "I love you too."

Chapter 15

We're on the highway headed west, but I'm unsure where. Rick wanted to celebrate me making it to my second trimester and asked if I would be down to trade in my Saturday morning jog with Rarity to do so. It was an easy yes. All I know is that Rick advised me to wear workout clothes and good sneakers. And to bring an extra change of clothes and socks as well.

Normally, I can't stand surprises. The uncertainty wrapped up in a surprise exasperates my anxiety. But, axe throwing showed me that Rick's surprises are interesting and fun.

I trust him.

"You ever think about how amazing it is that all the cars around us have people with their own unique and complex stories?" Rick asks me.

"Yeah! I believe the word for that is sonder. What's wild to me is that God knows all of those people down to the most minute detail. That blows my mind."

"Facts."

"So, I've been thinking about our time axe throwing last month."

"What about it?" Is it my imagination, or did his voice just become a little higher than its normal pitch?

"Well, I shared that you and Gaelle are kind of my only Christian friends right now, and I want that to change. I would love to have a squad of sisters to read the Bible and pray with. I just don't know how to make that happen."

"I think that's a God-given desire, Nin. And I'm pretty sure you're not the only woman who feels this way. What you need is a way to cast a wide net and see which fish you catch." He thinks for a moment. "Have you thought about doing a general ask on social media?"

That hadn't even occurred to me, but it's a great idea. "I like that idea. I could post in my stories on Instagram and use their polling function!"

He nods. "That sounds good. Do you want to do it now?"

"Now?"

"I know it's a little anxiety-inducing to put yourself out there like that, but there's no better time than the present."

Crap, he's right. I take a deep breath. "Okay, I'm going to do it!"

"Yas! You got this. Let me pray for you and this venture."

"That would be great."

"Father, we thank You for adopting us and bringing us into Your family. Lord, we're not called to walk this life of faith alone. I pray You will give Nin the courage to make this post. I pray that the right women will see it. I ask, Holy Spirit, that You would already be giving other women this same desire for fellowship, and Nin's step of faith would be an answer to their prayers. In Jesus's Name, amen."

"Amen. Okay. This'll take a few minutes."

"No worries."

After thinking for a moment, I decide to make this post one with no frills, a simple aesthetic. I type out: "Hey all, I'm thinking of starting a Bible study/prayer group. Let me know if you'd like to be a part of it." Then I add two polling options: "I'm interested in joining" and "I'm good, thanks". Once it's up, I close and uninstall the app because I don't want to be checking it for notifications.

"Done." I'm proud of myself.

"And we're almost there." I glance up to see us taking the exit for Waterdown Road.

"Am I good to know where we are now?"

He shakes his head. "Nah, you've waited so well for the last hour, you can make it another five minutes. Just enjoy the scenery."

I cross my arms and pretend to pout. "Just tell me already!"

He laughs at my misery. "Sorry, I thought I was driving Ruthia, not Cynthia."

At that, I snort. "Fine, fine," I take in all the trees and greenery around us. It piques my curiosity as it doesn't feel like we're in a major city or suburb, but it also doesn't feel rustic and country either. Within a few minutes, we make a left into an empty parking lot.

"Nice. I'm thankful that you're so used to waking up early in the morning. If we had come here even a few hours later, this would be packed." He parks at the far end of the parking lot.

"Now, are you going to tell me?"

"You'll figure out where we are as soon as we leave the parking lot." I roll my eyes playfully and then leave the car and follow his lead.

We're walking on a dirt path into a forest when I hear the faint sound of rushing water. Then I see a sign that says: 'Smokey Hollow'. A few more steps and I see the source of the sound I am hearing: a waterfall.

I rush to the landing overlooking the waterfall from the top and gasp at how beautiful it is.

"Oh, my goodness, you took me to a waterfall! Rick, this is so cool!" I embarrass myself at my volume until I remember that we're the only ones here.

"I'm glad you like it."

"Love. Not like, love!" I do my best Timone voice from The Lion King. His shoulders move up and down as he laughs.

Then we turn our attention back toward the waterfall. I lean against the railing of the landing and let the sound wash over me. I feel at peace. I wish I could get closer to it. After a little while of taking it in, I pull out my phone to capture a few pictures.

"I know a better spot for pictures. We can go to the base of the waterfall if you're up for it." Now his clothing instructions make sense.

"Is it a difficult trek?"

He shakes his head no. "It's pretty much stairs to the bottom and then we have to walk on rocks in the creek."

"That sounds very doable." Especially with the energy that has returned in this new trimester. "Let's go!"

I follow him to a stair walkway that looks to be attached to the Bruce Trail. As he said, it's fairly easy to navigate. All around we're surrounded by trees and the sounds of the forest, so relaxing. After about ten minutes, the walkway becomes a dirt path. "Hey, just be a bit more careful where you step now, Nin. You're wearing the right shoes, so there should be enough grip, but I don't want you to lose your footing."

"Gotcha Rick." I follow his directions, and pretty soon we're at the creek. Interspersed throughout are large rocks.

"Now, we're going to move from rock to rock to the base."

I try my best to follow his lead, the rocks he walks on and how long he stays on each one, but then I slip on one of them. I'm about to fall into the creek onto sharp rocks.

"Rick!" I call out and then I feel his hand on my arm. I look up to see that he's planted firmly on one rock and has a determined look on his face. With little effort, he pulls me up on the same rock that he's on.

"Are you okay? Do you want to go back?" His voice is laced with concern.

"I do not want to go back. I am a little shaken, but otherwise, I'm good. Thanks for helping me out there." I notice that his hand is still on my arm. He must notice at the same time as I do because he quickly moves his arm away and gestures further ahead.

"You're welcome. Hopefully, the most exciting part of the trip will be the waterfall and not the trek to get there." I chuckle.

"Agreed."

The sound of the rushing water becomes louder and louder as we get closer to the base, and then we're there.

It's breathtaking.

"Wow." It's the only word I can say.

We stay where we are for a few moments, just taking it in. It's not just the beauty of the waterfall that's hitting me, but everything surrounding it. It's hemmed in by two clefts of rocks that have beautiful greenery growing on them. I'm stunned at how what seems to be an inhospitable environment for life displays it so much.

It's like I can hear the Lord saying that this is true about my current situation as well. This pregnancy was supposed to take me out, derail my plans, and lead me to turn away from the Lord. Instead, my community has expanded and I'm experiencing more intimacy with Him than before.

I take out my phone for a few photos; he is right about this being the better spot. Once I'm done, he leans over to me and says something, but I struggle to hear him over the water.

"What did you say?!"

He leans in closer, his mouth right by my ear. I shiver at his nearness. "Want to go to the back of the waterfall?"

I don't trust myself to speak, so I simply nod. He tilts his head toward the waterfall and then walks in the water to a hill of packed dirt that's on a slight incline. It leads to an opening that's behind the waterfall.

This part is a bit more difficult for me. After slipping a few times trying to get up, Rick holds out his hand to me. I take it gratefully, and he pulls me up. I'm able to make it the last little of the way with my strength, which throws Rick off balance. This throws me off balance, too. He ends up pushed against the wall at the back of the waterfall with me having fallen flush against him, my head at his shoulder.

He steadies himself and then moves his arm around my waist to do the same for me. After a few moments, he hasn't removed his hands. I lean my head against his chest and hear his heartbeat going at a crazy pace.

"Roderick, what are we doing?"

"Honestly, Ruthia, I don't know." He gently pushes me backwards. I look up at his face and see that he's flustered, running his hands through his hair. It only occurs to me just now that I've never seen him stressed before.

"How about we sit?"

I nod at his suggestion. We plant ourselves in the dirt and it's amazing how loud this silence is. I choose to focus on the Falls and enjoy the spray and mist of it on me. I hear him turn to face me, and I follow suit.

"Ruthia, you're amazing." My cheeks warm. "From the moment I met you, I thought you to be gorgeous and, if possible, you've only become more attractive to me as I've gotten to know you. You're wise and fun and so strong. The times of the day I look forward to the most are when we spend time together. I don't know how else to say this, but I'm falling for you. I know that you're in a vulnerable time, so I've been trying to push these feelings away, but I don't think I can do that anymore. I just needed to be honest with you." He stops there, his face looking simultaneously hopeful and in agony.

I'm letting all his words - and their implications - hit me when I see the hope vanish from his eyes. I'm about to respond when he speaks again. "It's okay if you don't feel the same way. I'm content to just be your friend if that's all you -"

"Rick, stop. You don't need to renege on the things you shared. I was just thinking."

He looks chagrined, but now there are wisps of hope present in his eyes again.

"I like you too." He smiles. "First, I was telling myself it was because I found you good-looking, and then I admitted to myself that I have a little crush on you, but I know I'm beyond that now. I have genuine feelings for you."

He takes my hand in his and intertwines his fingers with mine. It feels so good, so lovely. I stare at our hands and take a deep breath, trying to get some courage for the next part I have to say.

"But I'm still figuring out things with my ex. Honestly, my heart is a bit of a mess."

"I know things are complicated, especially since you must consider your unborn child."

"Exactly! And you deserve an uncomplicated relationship." I start to take my hand away, but he does not let go.

"You don't get to tell me what I deserve, Nin. Unless you're talking about hell and eternal condemnation. In salvation, I've already gotten better than I deserve. Every other good thing in my life is a bonus, including being in a relationship with you." His eyes are so serious, so sincere, that it makes me cry.

He puts his arm around me and asks, "Is this okay?" I nod and lean into him, resting my head on his shoulder. He tightens his grip, now holding me with more confidence. "Feel free to use my shirt as a tissue." I take him up on his invitation and dry my eyes.

"Sorry about that."

"You never have to apologize for crying, Nin. It's a privilege to be trusted with your tears." He takes his arm from being around me, to my dismay. But at least he maintains his closeness to me and hasn't moved away.

"You really want to be with me? With all the baggage I come with?" I stare at the rushing water in front of us, needing reassurance.

"Yes." His voice is so sure as he puts a few fingers under my chin and turns my face to look at him. Then he cups one side of my face. "Ruthia, I want you in whatever way I can have you. If you're open to something more, I'll go as slow and give you as much time as you need."

I lean into his hand and sigh. "You're saying all the right things. If I didn't know you better, I would be skeptical. But I know you mean your words."

"I do." He winks at his choice of words. What would it be like to one day hear him say those words at an altar? My stomach flips at the thought.

"I'm not ready to be in a relationship with you yet. And please don't take this as a copout, but I just need to pray about this.".

He nods "I wouldn't want you to decide to be with me without prayer. Your faith is the thing I like the most about you, Nin. I'll be praying too. Would you be okay if we officially called today a date?"

"Okay," I smile.

"Okay." He returns it with one of his own.

We spend a few moments like that, just looking into each other's eyes and smiling. Then I hear my stomach rumble.

So embarrassing.

"Let's get some breakfast. There's a farmer's market close by that should be starting around now. Sound good to you?"

I nod, and we're off; down the little hill, through the pool, walking on top of the rocks and ascending back to the landing. It's not long before we're at the parking lot.

Within a few moments, we arrive at the farmer's market.

We get some cinnamon spice donuts from a vendor called Baked by Batches. Then, we get some berries from R.C. Farms. We peruse other vendors until Rick stops us at Fresh Market Farms. There, they are selling bouquets of flowers.

"Which one do you like?"

I survey the spread before us. "I'm very flower ignorant. They're all beautiful to me."

A lady at the stand comes over to us. "I just overheard you. One way to decide is to go by the meanings of the flowers. What would you want this trip to signify?"

"Hope or new beginnings?" Rick looks at me to see if I agree, and I nod.

"I know just what to do for you." She gathers white roses, another white flower, and small blue flowers. It's simple but beautiful and feels like me.

She hands it to Rick, who pays her for it. When they're done, he turns his attention back to me.

"To new beginnings, Nin." He holds one of my hands while offering me the bouquet. I gladly take it.

"Thank you, it's beautiful."

We exchange smiles. "Permission to keep holding your hand?"

"Granted."

We enjoy the farmer's market for the rest of the morning, and he doesn't let go of my hand for a moment.

I don't want him to.

We finally decide to head home, enjoying a comfortable silence as we drive back. It's then that I re-download Instagram to see if anyone has responded.

Six girls have responded. I shriek. It's a testament to Rick's training that his driving is unaffected. "That was a joyous sound, right? What are we celebrating?"

"Some women responded to my post!" The excitement I feel is making my voice louder than it needs to be. I try to dial it back a notch.

"Praise God! Who are they?"

"Well, there's Gaelle, who you know. Michelle who's my future boss. Hope, a girl that used to go to my old church, and three girls from your church: Eleora, Amy. and Cassandra.

"Wow, that's some group."

"Yeah, it looks to be such a random mashup of people and yet, I feel ..." I search for the word. "Peace. Like this deep assurance that these are the women God's chosen, and it will be good."

"Looks like you have two new beginnings from

today." He gives me a look of pure happiness, his smile reaching his eyes.

"Look at the road, military man!" He laughs but listens to me.

"There's a word for my distraction just now, but it's from the days before I followed Christ."

I'm curious. "Let's hear it."

He blushes, "Being booty blinded."

I laugh, hard. So hard that I snort multiple times. He joins in my laughter and then takes one of my hands in his while driving with the other. Then, slowly, he brings my hand to his mouth and gives it the sweetest of kisses.

I shiver as he brings it back down and sets our hands back on my knee.

For the rest of the drive, I try to just enjoy being with Rick. It takes concentrated effort not to engage all the confused thoughts of who I should be with.

His voice interrupts my thoughts. "Normally, I'd be walking my date to their front door, but I'm unsure what to do since we technically live together."

"Well, how about we decide that our date ends once we get to the apartment door?"

"That works." And that's what we do. When we reach the door, he opens his arms up for a hug, and I happily step into them. I feel cherished and safe in his embrace. When we break the hug, he leans over and gives me a kiss on my right cheek.

My heart flips at the brief contact of his lips against my skin, and the air between us charged. I'm so aware of my attraction to him and yet content.

"Thank you for a legit amazing date."

He smiles at my words. "I can honestly say that it

was my pleasure. See you at dinner?"

"Bet. See you then."

Then we enter the apartment and go our separate ways.

As soon as I shut my door, I flop on my bed and call Gaelle.

"Thia? What's up?" She sounds groggy.

"Did I wake you? It's, like, noon."

"Let me live my life. What's up?"

"I just got back from a date with Rick, and I don't know what to do."

"Wait, you didn't tell me it was a date!" She sounds awake now.

"Well, it became one partway through after he confessed his feelings for me."

She squeals at my revelation.

"You seem excited about this. Does that mean you think I should be with him? I don't know what to do, Elle! I like him and could see myself falling in love with him. But I know I still love Shane and that he wants to marry me. Help!" My words come out in a rush and I hyperventilate.

"Whoa. Breathe, ma chère, breathe. I think we gotta go old school with this, Ruthia. You need to fast and pray."

Yes. She's right!

"You're brilliant. I need to pray about this more and be able to quiet myself to hear God's voice and what His will is."

"Amen! Listen, Thia, both are great guys. I want you to know that I'm not Team Rick or Team Shane, okay? I'm Team God's Will For Your Life, so I'll be praying for you too."

"Thanks, best friend. I think I'll start with three weeks and see what God says then. If the Spirit impresses me to continue, then I will."

I have no doubt that this is what I'm supposed to do and that I'll hear God speak.

I just have no idea what He's going to say.

Chapter 16

Tears are in my mom's eyes as she sees me in my graduation gown and hat. "I am so proud of you."

"Thanks, Mom! I'm proud of me too."

"Let's get going before you make me cry," We exit the building to go outside.

I scan for my people and see Gaelle, Rick, Cynthia, and Rarity standing together in the shadow of a tree. Smart move. For an early June day, it is exceptionally warm. I point them out to my mom, and we walk toward them.

"Those are the people you've been living with?" I nod in response.

To my surprise, she greets Rarity with a hug. "Thank you for taking care of my baby."

Rarity hugs her back. "It has been my delight. You've raised a remarkable young woman. Here's my baby!" She moves Cynthia from behind her to in front of her. It looks like she's feeling shy.

My mom squats down to her level. "It's nice to meet you. My name is Emiline, but most people call me Em."

"My name is Cynthia, but you can call me Thia if

you want."

"Thank you!" My mom offers her a hand for a handshake. Cynthia shakes it with pride. "Mommy Ruthia looks so much like you. I love her so much, and I'm so glad that she is staying with us." It seems like Cynthia is no longer feeling shy.

"I second that." At Rick's words, my mom stands back up to take him in. In khakis and an olive-green dress shirt, he looks even more handsome than usual. "It's a privilege to meet you, ma'am. My name is Roderick, I'm Rarity's younger brother." He holds out his hand to shake hers.

"Ahh, it's lovely to meet you, too."

"Hi, Tante Em." Gaelle cuts in and goes to hug my mom.

"Gaelle, it is so nice to see you! My daughter is blessed to have so many wonderful people in her life." Here come the tears again. Oh boy.

"I think the ceremony is going to start soon. I should get in line with the other grads."

"Go! The four of us will find some seats." With Rarity's assurance, I feel free to part ways with them. I can't help feeling sad that my dad didn't come. I don't know if he'll ever want anything to do with me again.

The ceremony is long as expected as our respective deans read out our names. When it's time for the computer programming grads to be announced, my heart beats faster. I'll be seeing Shane in person for the first time in a couple of months! To no one's surprise, he looks handsome as he receives his diploma from his dean. I see him scan the room until his gaze lands on me. I receive a warm smile and can't help but smile back.

When my name is called, my mom disregards the 'hold your applause for the end' directions and cheers for me in a loud voice. I laugh as I'm handed my diploma and my dean chuckles along with me.

Once the ceremony ends, everyone rushes outside to find their families and take pictures.

While Rarity grabs a few photos of my mom and me, my mom starts waving her arms wildly.

"Shane!"

Oh, she's trying to catch his attention. Once she does, he walks over to us with his parents. My chest tightens. How is this going to go?

My mom goes to give him a hug, "I didn't know that you went here too until I heard your name inside. You've grown so much! I remember when you were this small." She holds out her hand to about half her height.

"It's great to see you too, Auntie Em!"

"Ruthia, congratulations." He's smiling, but I can see his nervousness in his eyes.

"Same to you, Shane!" I'm speaking too loudly because I'm nervous too.

"Oh! How about we get some pictures of you two together?" Shane and I exchange nervous glances, but there's no way to get out of my mom's suggestion since his parents agree.

Obediently, we stand together with a bit of space between us.

"Oh gosh guys, move closer to each other!"

At his mom's encouragement, we both scoot toward each other and his arm goes around my waist.

I forgot what it felt like to be this near to him.

It takes so much self-control to not lean into him.

As we smile for the pictures, he whispers to me, "You look beautiful, Thia. I've missed you."

"You clean up nice, but I already knew that." I get such a thrill at making him laugh.

Finally, our moms are content, and we can part ways.

"Who's in your entourage? I only know Gaelle."

"Oh, a few friends." I'm purposefully vague. He raises his eyebrow at my lack of information. Then he plasters a cordial smile on his face and walks toward Rarity and Roderick. I'm about to go run interference when his mom comes up to me.

"Hello, dear Thia! Congratulations!"

"Hi, Auntie!"

"I know you'll be successful in your chosen field. You were always so great with the kids at church and that was without the training you've now received.".

I smile at her encouragement. "Thank you for your kind words. By God's grace, I have a job that I'm starting on Monday!"

She claps for me. "Shane is in between two employers who are trying to nab him for their company. It's such a blessing that you'll both have income for the future." She says this last part meaningfully, with a quick glance at my belly. But her eyes hold a gentle warmth, no judgment or condemnation to be found.

"You're right. God is good."

"All the time. And all the time..."

"God is good." We exchange smiles.

"Now, let me get my son. I need pictures with him too! Shane!" He turns around at the sound of her voice.

It's weird to see him and Rick next to each other. My looming decision is literally in front of me. Shane is taller, but Rick is more built. They're both too handsome for their own good.

When it looks like all the photo-taking is done, I excuse myself to go return my gown. To my surprise, Shane joins me in line.

"Hey, how did you meet that family? Do they go to your church?"

"I don't want to get into it right now, Shane."

"So, not from church, then?"

Now I'm annoyed. "I told you I didn't want to talk about it."

There's a beat of silence. "I'm sorry. I should've listened to you. I was letting myself be led by insecurity and fear rather than respect for your boundary."

I let out an enormous sigh, but I can't help the smile that comes from his apology. "I accept your apology. Why were you feeling afraid and insecure?"

He looks thoughtful. "I guess I'm wondering if Roderick is the reason we aren't back together yet."

I don't know what answer I was expecting, but that wasn't it. I could change the subject, but he was honest with me. I can reciprocate that. "To be honest, yes, there's the potential of something with him. But I'm still trying to figure everything out."

"Thanks for your honesty, Thia," he says and then puts a hand on my shoulder. I look up at him in surprise. "I love you, Thia."

Those words bring me both elation and sadness. I hate that words I used to treasure now cause me pain.

"I love you too, Shane. I just don't think love is enough."

"I need your trust, right?"

He remembers what I said before. I nod my head, and we've reached the front of the line. We return our gowns and walk back toward our people, who are all chatting with each other. Our conversation seems to have ended when Shane turns to me.

"Thia?"

"Mhmm?"

"Would it be okay if I hugged you?"

Once again, he's surprised me. Before I can overthink it, I respond, "Sure, why not?" I add a shrug to feign nonchalance, but my tapping foot betrays my nervous disposition.

We stop walking and he opens up his arms. I step into them and barely hold back a contented sigh at his touch. My body is so used to seeing him as a haven of safety. I resist the urge to cuddle against him and instead step back. It's one of the shortest hugs we've ever had and, yet it felt incredibly long.

"Well, bye, I guess!" I'm proud that I kept my voice steady, as if that hug didn't unlock something hidden inside me.

He waves back and heads over to his parents. I walk back to my group, a storm of emotions that calms down when Rick catches my eye. "You okay?" He mouths to me.

I nod my head. His awareness of and concern for me has a settling effect. To be seen so clearly reminds me of how God sees me in all of this. It's almost been almost a week into the fast, and I have not received an obvious answer. Yet, I have been experiencing more intimacy with God as I'm praying more. I know I just have to trust that He will tell me what to do.

Easier said than done.

Chapter 17

After taking a deep breath to ease some of my anxiety, I start the Zoom call. It's been a couple of weeks since the six girls responded to my invitation for a women's accountability/Bible study group. After coordinating everyone's availability, we're meeting for the first time.

As soon as I start the call, I see all six of them in the waiting room: Eleora, Amy, Gaelle, Cass, Michelle, and Hope.

I admit them all and soon see their faces in their respective rectangles.

"Hey everyone! So, to be honest, I don't really have an agenda for today other than having the chance to get to know each other more. We can share our names, what life looks like for us right now physically, emotionally, and spiritually, and why we joined this group. I can start us off." I pause just in case anyone wants to say anything, but no one unmutes.

"So, physically, I am very aware of my pregnant-ness. While I have some of my energy back, I still just feel not normal. Emotionally, I'm a hot mess. I don't know whether God wants me to be with my baby daddy or this new guy in the picture that seems wonderful in nearly every way. Spiritually, I think God and I are good. I'm just trying to figure out what He wants for my life. But I'm definitely looking for more community, and that's why I started this group."

"I can go next." I smile at Gaelle's willingness to go next. "My name is Gaelle, and I am close friends with Ruthia. Physically, I'm good other than starting my period, which always sucks." Everyone nods their heads. "Emotionally, I'm okay. Not great, but not awful either. I just feel pretty neutral, I guess? And spiritually, I'm feeling distant. I don't know why, but I'm not experiencing any closeness or passion in my relationship with God. I joined this group because I could use a group of girlfriends. There are not many people my age at my church and during the school year, I'm often in a Bible study on my campus, but that stops in the summer. I'm realising how much I need community."

"Thanks for sharing, Elle. I think we may have all gone through periods of lacking that oomph in our relationship with God. That's very relatable."

Gaelle smiles at my words and then we're silent, waiting for the next person to speak.

"Well, I'll have to go, eventually. It might as well be now. So, hey everyone, I'm Hope. Physically, I'm drained. The life of a single mother is exhausting. I got pregnant a few years ago by an abusive ex and currently live a few hours away from the GTA in Ajax because it's cheaper, but that means less support. Emotionally, I'm also drained. I think giving all I have to a little human is such hard work, and I feel stretched thin. Spiritually, I know God is good, but I don't feel it. I have no real friends at the moment since I'm still looking for a church out here, so I jumped at the opportunity of this group. I know that Ruthia's love for the Lord means she'll create a life-giving space that honours God, which is what I need. Thank you, guys, for being willing to meet now. This is naptime and one of the few times that I'm available."

At Hope's words, Amy unmutes herself. "We are happy to accommodate you. Being a single mom is like being a superhero. I've been raised by one, and I'm so appreciative of her."

"Having to be both parents is a huge undertaking. You're doing a phenomenal job, I'm sure." Cass adds.

"Thanks, everyone. Not me crying at y'all being so kind." Hope wipes at her eyes as we all chuckle.

"Well, I'm unmuted, so I can share next. My name is Amy. Physically, I'm feeling strong. I'm training for a half marathon, so there's that. Emotionally, I'm all over the place. One day, I'm super happy and have all this zeal and motivation. The next day, I struggle to get out of bed. I do not know what's wrong with me, and it feels like I'm going crazy sometimes. Spiritually, it also feels up and down: days when I'm super in love with God and then days where I'm doubting whether Christianity is even true." Amy pauses and we all nod our heads encouragingly. "I don't think I've ever really said that aloud, but it's true." She starts to tear up. "I don't know what's wrong with me, I guess. I'm also a hot mess. But I think Ruthia seems like a cool person, and I thought it wouldn't hurt to give a group like this a try."

"Oh, honey," Cass's voice is warm. "Thanks for sharing."

"Yes. Also, this sounds like you're under some spiritual warfare. I'm not sure what you believe theologically about that, but it sounds like the enemy is attacking you." Count on Gaelle to bring up spiritual warfare!

"I didn't think of that before. But what do I do? How do I fight back?"

My answer is automatic. "Well, we've gotta wear the full armour of God first. That's how we withstand attacks."

"Facts. Let me pull up my notes from a sermon I heard on it a few months ago." Gaelle pauses to look for the sermon. "Here it is. He gave us these questions to reflect upon: How is truth holding you up? How is Christ's righteousness protecting your heart? How is your salvation covering your mind? Are your footsteps following peace? How can you be growing in your faith in Jesus?"

"That's so good. Can you share that with us somehow?"

Gaelle nods in response to Michelle's request.

"And then, for fighting back. The key here is knowing the Word of God and wielding it the way Jesus did when Satan tempted Him." Hope says.

"Amen. That's a good word. Also, prayer is a way we fight back. Praying for God's will to be done, not the enemy's." Michelle adds.

Everyone is nodding their head now.

"Well, I love the direction that our conversation took. Thanks everybody for participating." Well, not everybody. "Eleora, is there anything you'd like to share? Would you be good to go next?" I try to be as gentle as possible.

She unmutes. "Sure. Hi everyone, I'm Eleora. I know I was being quiet; I was just content to listen to y'all talk and glean from all the wisdom. I just became a Christian a few months ago, so I'm still learning a lot. Physically, I'm alright. I'm inspired by Amy doing a marathon. Emotionally, I'm not great. My mom and I are estranged, and her birthday just passed. It was hard not celebrating it with her. I miss her, but she also has some toxic qualities, and I don't think it's healthy to be in a relationship with her. I also am about to enter my last high school exam week and that feels crazy. There's a lot of sadness over this chapter of my life ending. Spiritually, I'm just in love with God and so thankful that He brought me back to Himself. I just want to grow in my faith, and that's why I figured I would join this kind of group."

Such a young believer! I live to see it. "We're so happy you're here." My words bring a bright smile to her face.

"And I'm sorry about the situation with your mom. That sounds hard." We all nod, agreeing with Michelle's sentiment.

"And now I'm crying. Thank you for saying that."

"Of course. I can share next. Physically, I'm just trying to hit my 7000 steps a day. Emotionally, I'm feeling lonely and resentful toward God. I guess that's spiritually too, isn't it? I'm same sex attracted, and it's hitting me as I'm in my mid-thirties that I won't have a family of my own one day. I guess I'm grieving that? I'm also angry with God about it because He let me have this sexual orientation, knowing that I wouldn't be able to act on it. Like, I know that life isn't only meaningful when you have a spouse and kids and that my hope is ultimately in Jesus, but I still wish I could have those things, too. It's a messy place to be."

I didn't know this about Michelle. Amy is the first to respond. "Wow, thanks for your vulnerability."

"Yeah, I can't imagine what living with that must be like for you. What has your journey of realizing this about yourself been like?" Gaelle asks.

"Well, I didn't have many crushes growing up. I just always had close relationships with other girls. Then, in Grade 8, I realized I wanted to be more than friends with one of those girls. I spent a lot of time hating myself for my desires and pushing them down. Then in high school, I dated different guys hoping for that to change me, but it didn't. I ended up sleeping with one of them, and it was a horrible experience. Consensual but painful and not enjoyable. That night ended up resulting in an abortion. After that, I just decided that I was done with pretending and embraced my sexual orientation. It's a longer story, but God met me in that place and brought me into relationship with him about 10 years ago. I've been celibate ever since."

"I so want to hear that story sometime! Like Amy said before, thank you for being so vulnerable. I appreciate you sharing your experience with us and welcome you doing so anytime." I want Michelle to know that her experience is welcome here.

"I was nervous to share, but everyone was just

being vulnerable, and it made me feel safe, I guess? Is it weird that I feel safe with you all, and we've only just met?"

"Not weird, but maybe God? I feel the same way." It's like Eleora took the words right out of my mouth.

"Yeah, thanks for creating this space for us, Ruthia."

Cass's affirmation makes me smile. "Aww, you guys. You're making me Black girl blush." I joke and we all laugh, even Amy, the only White person present.

"Well, I think that I'm the last one. My name is Cassandra, but you all can call me Cass. Physically, I've been emotionally eating lately and gaining weight, so that sucks. Emotionally, I'm feeling better now that it's summer, and I can relax a bit from school. But, things are still hard because I'm completely in love with my guy best friend but don't want to risk our friendship by revealing these feelings. Whenever we're together, I'm a mess inside. Spiritually, I'm just trying to trust God through it. And I want to join this group because I would love accountability in my walk with God."

I nod my head in empathy. "Definitely experienced the whole liking my best friend thing. It sucks." I remember those months when my feelings were growing for Shane before he told me that he liked me. My heart pangs at the memories.

Cass sighs. "It really does."

I give a moment of silence before moving forward. "Well, I guess we've all introduced ourselves and shared together. There seems to be safety built within this group, which I love. Based on our spiritual warfare discussion, being in the Word and in prayer are key things. Maybe that's what this group can be for?"

Amy unmutes herself again. "That sounds great." Everyone else gives a variation of a thumbs up or a nod of agreement.

"Great, well then, if everyone could send me their cell numbers, I can make a group chat on WhatsApp for us. Also, we need a name." The women look excited and thoughtful at my declaration to name ourselves.

"Well, there seems to be a theme of messiness from all of our sharings." Gaelle's right, that's something we all seem to have in common.

"How about Hot Messies?"

I toss Michelle's suggestion around my mind. I like it.

"I like the play on words because it's like hot misses, but with the vowels flipped," Eleora says.

"Can we make hot, hawt? Like, h a w t? That might be extra, but I think it's fun."

Amy claps her hands at Hope's idea. "I love that so much!"

"Same!" Cass's excitement is apparent.

"Okay, we've reached a consensus. We are the Hawt Messies." I say with a dramatic flair, and everyone cheers.

I can just tell this is the start of something great.

Chapter 18

I'm just getting on the bus to head home from work when my phone vibrates in my pocket. I check it to see who it is and see that it's a call from my mom. She's probably calling to see how work was. It's been a week of adjusting and getting in rhythm, but I'm feeling more at home in the role now, and the kids have become comfortable with me. I look forward to giving her this report!

"Hey Mommy, what's up?"

"It's Shane." A chill goes down my spine. Is this how God is going to answer my prayer? Through a divine word from my mom?

"What do you mean it's Shane?"

"The ex-boyfriend and the baby's father. It's him, right?"

"Yes, but I thought you didn't want to know. How did you figure it out?"

"Shane came over today and revealed himself."

I nearly drop my phone. "What?!" I try to keep my voice down, but I still get strange looks from the other passengers on the bus.

"Well, I guess you told him that your dad isn't at

the church office on Mondays?"

"Yep, he would know that because that's why we never spent time together there on Mondays. But forget that. You're killing me here. Tell me what happened!"

"Well, he knocked on the door, and I answered it, surprised to see him. He said that he wanted to speak with both of us. We went to the living room since your father was relaxing in the recliner. He greeted your dad and asked if he could sit on the couch and talk to us. We said yes. Then he told us he was the guy you'd been dating and the baby's father."

"Oh, my goodness. What happened next? Did Daddy hit him?" I remember the slap all too well.

"He sure looked like he wanted to, but he didn't." I release the breath that I didn't realize I'd been holding.

"He accused him of conspiring with his parents, aiming to disgrace the family and ruin his reputation within the church."

"Wow, he found a way to make it about himself." I'm not even sure if I'm more frustrated or sad.

"Shane then denies that and tells him that his parents didn't know either. Then Shane shares that he loves you, wants to marry you, and wants our blessing." I gasp. I know that he's said that before, but it's one thing to mention marriage and another to ask for parental permission.

"At this, your father goes ballistic and says some things that I'd rather not repeat."

"Is it coarse language?"

"No."

Then why would she want to hide it from me?

Realization dawns. "He said something negative regarding me, didn't he?" My mom's silence is all the confirmation I need.

"It's okay, Mom, you can tell me. I want to know where he's at in his thoughts of me."

She sighs. "If you say so. He said that he has no daughter, so he has no blessing to give."

I push away the tears. I asked for this.

"Then what happened?"

"Well, then Shane gets angry! He tells him you're a beautiful, godly, intelligent and amazing person and that it's a privilege for anyone to say that you're their daughter."

My heart melts at these words. Now I want to cry for a different reason.

"And then?"

"So, then your dad tells him to get out, and I walk Shane to the door. I thank him for telling us, and I give him my blessing to marry you, but only if that's what you want. And then I called you."

"Thanks, Mommy. This was important for me to know. What do you think I should do?"

"I don't know. Roderick is a godly gentleman. I would happily call him my son one day. Shane has made mistakes, but his love for God and you have been without a doubt. But even if I could choose between them, I wouldn't tell you my choice. You have to hear from God."

"I've been trying to hear him! This coming Sunday will mark the end of the three weeks of fasting I've been doing, and I still feel torn."

"Hmm. Well, my only advice is maybe to spend some time with Shane. You see Roderick every day, which gives him an extra advantage."

"You're not wrong. Okay, I'll call him."

"Okay, Ruthia. I love you so much and am proud to say that I'm your mom!"

Her words ease the pain caused by my dad. "Thank you. I love you too! Bye!" She hangs up, and then I take a deep breath for courage. Before I can chicken out, I tap on Shane's icon on my phone to call him. It rings twice before he answers.

"Thia?"

"Shane, my mom just told me everything that happened! What were you thinking?!" My voice is loud and angry. Once again, I receive strange looks from the other people on the bus at my outburst.

"I want to be the responsible man of integrity that God has called me to be, and that means doing uncomfortable stuff, like talking with your parents." His voice is steady.

"He could've hurt you, Shane." My voice is small. That's the real reason I'm upset. I was afraid for his safety because I love him so much still.

"I'm fine, Ruthia. Why did you think I'd be in danger? I know he has a temper. But do you think that your dad would get physically violent?"

I don't know how to answer that question.

"Wait, have you seen him get violent?" His voice is incredulous.

I remain quiet.

"Thia, do not tell me he's physically harmed you." He sounds angry now, but protectively so.

"Then I won't tell you."

"I ought to go back there and give him a piece of my mind!"

"Shane, no. Don't pull a Will Smith and fight a battle that I didn't ask you to fight."

He lets out a frustrated sigh. "Okay. Fine. Could we meet up, though?"

I think about it for a moment. Based on what he's done today, I think it warrants seeing him in person.

"Sure, whereabouts?"

"Let's do Mystic?" I smile at his suggestion for our favourite place to get Caribbean food. "Do you think you'd enjoy that type of food tonight? And are you able to get there? Do I need to pick you up?"

"Chill fam, I'm on the number one bus right now. I'll just get off at Kennedy and take the Kennedy bus down. I should be there in about 30 minutes, at worst 45."

"Okay, see you there. And, thanks."

"For what?"

"For agreeing to this date. Love you, bye!" He hangs up before I can tell him it's not a date. But is that true? We're meeting together, alone, he's probably paying and there's romantic interest present.

It's a date.

But what does this mean about Roderick? How would he feel about me going on this date with Shane? He was sweet about graduation and didn't even mention Shane being there. But now? I don't know. We haven't been on a date together since the waterfall almost three weeks ago, although my mom was right in saying that I see him every day, so we end up spending a lot of time together, anyway.

I push away these thoughts and pay attention to the bus stops. Soon enough, I'm coming off the Kennedy bus and walking toward the restaurant.

When I get in, Shane already has a table for us.

My heart can't help but flip when I see him. Even in just a hoodie and jeans, he's so handsome.

I walk over to his table and sit down across from him.

"Hey. I'm glad that you came. I entertained the notion of you bailing on me."

"You know me better than that. I wouldn't do that to you." I shrug off my cardigan. It's hot in here.

"Yeah, but I would deserve it if you did." He looks sad now.

"Hey, I told you I already forgive you for everything."

He nods. "You're right. You did."

"I could get used to hearing those first two words." I tease, and he chuckles. The tension leaves his body, and it's nice to see him relaxed.

It's nice to be here with him.

"Do you want to do our usual?" he asks me.

"Yep. When the waitress comes, feel free to order." I relax in my seat.

Soon enough, the waitress arrives and Shane orders two pineapple pops, one jerk chicken fried rice, a jerk chicken chow mein, and four skewers for our appetizers: chicken, beef, lamb, and shrimp. As he says each item, I feel my stomach rumble.

Fasting is hard.

"So, tell me about your day."

"It was pretty good. I'm working at a daycare near the mall, in the same civic center as the library. It's been about a week now and I feel like I'm more used to the schedule and systems that Michelle has in place. She's my boss and the owner of the daycare."

He smiles at the information I share. "That's great. How did you end up getting this job? I don't remember you having your practicum there."

"That's a much longer story." The waitress comes with our drinks, giving me a chance to delay answering by drinking my pineapple pop. And then I realize that I trust him enough to share all that's happened.

"Please, go on. I want to know everything that I've missed in your life over the last two months."

"Well, then. When you broke up with me, I decided to get an abortion." He looks surprised.

"But you've always been pro-life." He's genuinely confused.

"Yeah, but I was hurt and angry, and this baby was the only person I could take my pain out on."

"So, what happened? What made you stop?"

"Do you remember that little girl that was at our graduation?" He nods. "She's the reason I'm still pregnant today. I was on my way to the clinic when I slipped on a ball she was playing with. Then she dragged me into the daycare to play with her for the day. That's the same daycare where I work now. My schooling and the way I was with the kids that day scored me the job. My boss also is a believer who had her own unexpected pregnancy years ago, so she was empathetic to my situation."

"Wow. Praise God for that little girl."

"I know, right? And well, now you probably know that I'm not living with my parents anymore." He nods. "I'm living with Cynthia, that's the little girl's name, and her mother, Rarity."

"Oh wow. You chose to live with strangers

instead of Gaelle?"

"I know it sounds crazy, but Rarity invited me over when she came to pick Cynthia up from daycare. That afternoon, we just clicked. She was also going through a tough time, and we bonded over that. She told me when I left that if there was any way she could help me, she would. So, when my dad kicked me out, her place was the first one to come to mind."

"And when did Roderick come into the picture?" I smirk at this question. His jealousy is evident on his face.

"Rick came to visit his sister soon after I started staying with them."

"So, you guys are living together?" I can tell that he's trying to keep his emotions in check.

"Yes - along with Rarity and Cynthia. We've become great friends."

He nods, looking relieved at the word 'friends'. He's about to say something else when the waitress comes with our skewers.

"Thank you!" She smiles at me and then heads over to the bar.

"I can pray for us," Shane offers, and I nod.

"Lord, thank you for this food and that we can be here together. Please bless our food, the hands who prepared it and our time together. Amen."

We're silent as we eat, and I can tell that he's thinking hard about something. Eventually, he breaks the silence. "I'm thankful for how God has kept you these last couple of months, even though I haven't been part of it."

I smile. "Yeah, He is good. Other than the time with my parents, what were you up to today?"

"I met with the company TD SYNNEX, accepting their job offer."

"Congratulations! I know nothing about that company, but I can tell that it's a big deal." I'm genuinely proud of him. He looks bashful.

"Thanks." He looks nervous now. "Thia, would you be willing to work through a questionnaire with me? It helps people decide if they're a good fit for marriage. We don't have to do it though if you don't want to."

I think hard about his request. Maybe this would help me with making my decision. "Sure!" He looks so grateful at my response; his smile reaches his eyes now. He takes out his phone and swipes at its screen.

"Okay, so the first section is on spiritual beliefs. A lot of these I think we already know about each other. I would love to talk about a few of them though, if that's good with you."

"Go for it."

"Alright, how would you define what marriage is? What is the biblical basis for your definition?"

"Hmm. From Ephesians 5, I think we get a fantastic definition of the purpose of marriage. It's supposed to be a tangible demonstration of the relationship between Christ and the church. Right?"

"Right. Like the church, the wife submits, and like Jesus, the husband sacrifices. Okay, the next section is about children. How many children do you want and how far apart would you like to space your children?"

"As an only child, I hundred percent want at least two. I'm not sure I want to go over four. And maybe a few years apart between each so that they can feel like they're growing up together. What about you?"

He thinks for a moment. "I like the idea of even numbers so that no one ever feels left out. So two or four work for me. Next up we have: what do you believe the Bible teaches regarding family planning methods? What methods of contraception are you knowledgeable about and comfortable with?"

"This I don't have an answer for. All I know for sure is that I want nothing abortive. Anything would have to prevent conception but shouldn't happen after conception."

He nods. "Yeah, I agree. Also, I think this is where the idea of stewardship comes in. Remember when Cor and Zara were talking about how God entrusts us with things to take care of well? I think that could apply to children. Like, how many can we afford to care for well?"

I nod. "I see where you're going with that train of thought. Considering stewardship, God probably wouldn't call some people to have 15 children, for they would be incapable of properly caring for them."

"Exactly. Okay, next one. If God gives you all the children you desire, would you pursue sterilization (vasectomy or tubal ligation)? If so, which form would you choose? I can answer this one first."

"Go ahead." I take this moment to polish off the lamb skewer.

"I'm down for getting a vasectomy. If you had to do a tubal ligation, it would be a major surgery. Why would I let you go through that when I could just go through a simple procedure? That just makes little sense to me." My heart warms at his answer.

"Thanks for that. I appreciate it."

"No problem. Anything you'd like to add?" I shake my head. Just then, the waitress comes with our meals. We thank her, and I tuck in while Shane reads the next question.

"Okay, if you could not have biological children, would you adopt? What age would you want to adopt them? Would you adopt from a different ethnicity or culture?"

"I would be down for that. I think no older than 5. And I'd want to adopt Black children, whether Caribbean or African."

Shane nods. "I agree. I never thought about the age question. What's your reasoning behind that number?"

"Oh! Children begin to have autobiographical memory at around 4 years old. I would love for them to have memories of us being their parents."

"Makes sense. Okay, what is your parenting philosophy, specifically regarding correction methods? Would you ever spank your children?"

My answer is immediate, and my voice is firm. "No. There are other ways to discipline children without physically hurting them."

"I don't disagree, Thia. I knew that's what you would say. Okay, the next few questions are about cultural background stuff. I don't think we need to discuss that. Ooh. Here's a good one: would you ever live with your parents or have them live with you? Why?"

"If either of your parents were widowed, and they were so old that they couldn't take care of themselves, I would have them live with us. I love your parents! My dad doesn't even consider me his daughter, so that's a nope. My mom, I'd be down, though."

"I'm sorry about your dad, Thia."

I try to brush him off. "Not your fault."

"But it kind of is, I should've stopped us from having sex. None of this would've happened otherwise."

"Then it would be my fault too, since I also didn't stop us. Plus, regardless. You're not the reason my dad apparently has anger problems. That's on him."

"You're right, and I agree with your response. Since we're both only children, we would have to be the ones to take care of our parents. Okay, some lifestyle questions. Are there certain countries, cities, places or communities you would never live in?"

"Nah. I'm good to go wherever God calls. Ideally, I wouldn't want to be too far from our families, but if God said move to India, my response is: what flight are we booking?"

"Although we pretty much already live in India," Shane says dryly, and I laugh. "I love the faith that you have, Thia. And I agree. For the next topics, we have to identify what would be non-negotiable or a deal-breaker."

"Kay, let's do this."

"Both of us working versus one of us working?"

"Not a deal breaker for me. I'm open to being a stay-at-home wife if we can afford it, and I feel like God is calling me to that."

"Sweet. Regularly taking vacations? I think this goes back to stewardship for me. If we are already being generous,

and we can afford to travel with our kids, then I'm down for that."

I nod. "Agreed. What's next?"

"Okay, how will we treat devices in our home? Are they allowed in rooms? How many TVs should we have?"

"I want a family that is close to each other and spends time together. With that in mind, I wouldn't want there to be TVs in the bedrooms but in a communal space. As the kids get older, sure, they can keep their phones in their rooms. But maybe other devices go to a common area? I don't know. I haven't thought about this before."

"I haven't either, but I think that's wise. Okay, finances. What level of debt or savings are you bringing into the marriage? What are your thoughts on credit cards and lines of credit? Okay, so I have a good amount of savings and no debt." He tells me.

I'm impressed. I didn't realize how good he was with money. "I have some debt, but I'll be able to pay it off in a few months since I'm now working full time and have no living expenses."

"Nice. Praise God for Rarity." I nod in agreement. "Okay, the next few finance questions can be summed up in this: will finances be separate or together? I grew up with my parents' finances combined. I would see them meet to discuss finances and pay bills together. I've always wanted that in a marriage. What are your thoughts on that?" He looks nervous. He has no reason to be, though.

"I agree. The Bible says that two become one. Why would we keep finances separate if we're one? That doesn't make sense to me."

He looks relieved. "Sweet. On education, what type of education do you desire for your children to have?"

"I feel like I went through the public school system and turned out okay. I don't see why we would need to send them to a private school."

"What about homeschooling?" He asks. "If it was anyone but you, I wouldn't even consider homeschooling. But you're so good with kids and a teacher at heart, I think you would be amazing for them."

"Hmm. Homeschooling does not seem appealing to me. But it's not a deal breaker for me."

"Okay, fair enough. Now, ummm. The next set of questions is about sex." He looks sheepish. I laugh.

"I think we've already crossed the point about being embarrassed about this, Shane." He laughs too.

"You're right. Are you both committed to learning what pleases the other person in love?"

Now I'm bashful. "Okay, you're right, that is a somewhat uncomfortable question."

"See!" We laugh together. "And my answer to the question is yes." His eyes take on a sensual expression that matches his words. I quickly drink some of my pop.

"Same. Although, I would love to talk with a pastor about what is and isn't okay. I feel like our culture just says that anything goes as long as it's consensual, but I don't know if that's what the Bible says."

"Cool, that's pretty much all the questions. How are you feeling?" Now done asking me things, he goes to town on his food.

"I appreciated them. They had me thinking of things I hadn't thought of before. Where did you get them?"

"From my dad. They were the questions he and my mom went through when they were discerning whether to get engaged. They know I want to marry you, but they want to make sure it's the wisest decision, so he gave me these to work through. I feel good about our answers and that we agree on a lot of things. That doesn't surprise me, though. I thought we'd be a good fit. This just proves it for me." He's so sincere. I can tell that he means every word.

"Well, I'm thankful that he gave them to you," I avoid the second part of what he said.

He doesn't let me. "And how has doing it influenced your thoughts about us?"

I sigh. "It shows that God could very well call us to be together, and it would be good. I just don't know if that's the case yet."

"That's fair. You want whatever God wants for you. I can't be mad about that." I can tell he's disappointed, but he's handling it well.

"Are you guys ready for your bills?"

We were so transfixed by each other that we didn't even realize our waitress had arrived.

"Sure, one bill please," Shane says before I can say otherwise. I glance at him, the question in my eyes of whether he really wants to pay for it. He nods.

"Okay, cash or card?" Shane goes through the motions of paying, which gives me a few moments to think.

I meant what I said. I could see a life with him; a good life. These questions showed that. I just wish I knew whether that was the life that God wanted for me.

"Thia, would you be comfortable with me driving you home?" His voice pierces through my thoughts.

"Sure, thank you." It hits me how much more I trust him now than even yesterday. I trusted him enough to tell him what's been going on. I trusted him enough to do this questionnaire. And I trust him enough to know where I now live.

We don't talk much on the way, other than me giving him directions to the building. When we get there, Shane exits his side to open my door for me.

It's giving big date energy.

Once I'm out, he walks me to the front door of the building. The doorman waves at me but looks at Shane with some suspicion. I smile at him to let him know that I'm good, and he smiles back.

"Well, thanks for dinner." I feel like my words are lame.

"Thank you for the privilege of a date. I love you, Ruthia." Maybe it's all we've talked about or the sincerity in his eyes, but I instinctively go to hug him and throw my arms around his neck. His arms go around my waist and I breathe him in. The familiarity of his embrace almost makes me cry. I forgot how at home I feel here.

"I love you too, Shane," I whisper into his chest. I'm not sure he can hear me.

He pulls us apart after a moment and the look in his eyes shows he heard my words. Then, he kisses me on the forehead and backs away from me.

"Have a good night."

"Same to you." I wait for him to drive off and when he's gone, I lean against the building doors.

"Lord. Please tell me your will."

Chapter 19

I'm back to the race.

Shane and Rick are coming around the corner, then Rick slows down at the last second, and Shane crosses the finish line first. He walks over to me to receive the trophy in my hands. As I give it to him, our hands touch and then the scene changes.

I watch Shane and Dream Ruthia wake up together by an alarm. It's Sunday morning. We are joking together as we get ourselves awake. We get ready, moving through a morning routine. He picks me up while I am unwrapping my hair, and I steal his towel while he is getting in the shower.

Then he goes downstairs to start breakfast while I go to a child's room. By the look of it, she's a girl. I pick out three outfits for her to choose from for church, and then I walk through an adjoining bathroom between their rooms and do the same for our son.

I stand in their bathroom and look at my little girl sleeping so peacefully. Then I feel arms wrap around me. Shane has snuck up behind me. He picks me up and sets me on the counter in their bathroom. I wrap my legs around his waist, and he puts his head on my shoulder, his beard hair tickling my neck. I try to stifle my giggles.

"Shane, honey, what are you doing?" I try to keep my voice low because the kids are still sleeping.

"Holding my wife. Maybe we should just stay in today? Go back to bed," he whispers in my ear, and I shiver.

"Pastor Shane Reid, you have a sermon to preach today, no? I don't think you can play hooky." He laughs.

"Okay, First Lady. You win."

"As always," I joke, and he lifts me off the counter.

"We will continue this later, though, Mrs. Reid." He kisses me on the forehead.

Then I lean up. "I'm counting on that, Mr. Reid."

I wake up and the dream continues to replay in my mind. I've had this dream before.

Months ago.

'It's not a dream; it's a vision of the future.' God's voice. Finally, he speaks.

"Lord, are you saying what I think you're saying? That I'm supposed to marry Shane?"

'Is the vision not clear enough?'

"No, it's pretty clear." I sigh. "What will I tell Rick?"

'The truth will set you free. And he belongs to me. I will take care of him as I always have.'

I can't help but cry. There was a part of me that wanted it to be Rick.

"If this was always the plan, why did you let

everything go the way it did? Why even introduce me to Rick at all?"

'Little children, guard yourselves from idols.'

Understanding sets in. This entire process was to make sure that Shane wouldn't be an idol in my life. I had to see him as a human capable of making mistakes and hurting me. I also had to recognize that my life didn't revolve around him and that I could be with someone else if God willed it.

Still, I feel an intense grief. But paradoxically, also an immense peace, peace that surpasses my understanding. I know I'm in God's will.

I grab my phone from my nightstand. It's only just after 11pm. A safe time to call my night owl best friend.

"Hey Thia, what are you doing up? Everything okay?"

I didn't plan what I was going to say, so I blurt out, "It's Shane."

"What do you mean? Is he okay?" Now she sounds worried.

"He's fine, or at least I think he is. I don't know. I mean, God answered. It's Shane."

"Oh wow. How are you feeling about his choice?"

"Bittersweet. But I think I was going to feel like this either way."

"That's understandable. Walk me through the sweet part of how you're feeling."

"Well, I think I was holding off on dreaming or anticipating a life with him because of the possibility of Rick. But now, I feel free to imagine a future with Shane; to be starting a family with him." As I speak, the joy in God's choice increases in me.

"Like, I'm happy to get back together with him. I want all that God has for us. He's the same guy I became such close friends and fell in love with. Except now, there's a humility and a gravity to him that wasn't present before. He'll be a good father. I know that we'll enjoy life together filled with laughter, joy, and growth in the Lord."

"I'm happy for you, best friend." She sounds like she's crying.

"Elle, you alright over there?"

"Oui, I just have been praying for you and wanting the best for you so much. To hear you sounding so confident and happy is an answer to my prayers. These are positive tears, mon amie."

"Thanks for being such a loving friend through all of this, Elle. I couldn't have made it through it without you."

"You're welcome. Now, how are you going to break the news?"

"To whom, Shane or Roderick?"

"Both."

"Hmm. I can tell Roderick the next time we run into each other. That's going to suck."

"And with Shane?"

"I don't know. Is this something I should communicate over the phone or in person? And what do I say? Do I just tell him I want to get back together or that I want to marry him?"

"Okay, maybe just tell him you'd like to see him? That way, you can meet in person, and you can have some time to think about everything."

"That's a good idea. Thank God tomorrow is

Saturday. Focusing on work would be difficult."

"Facts. Are you going to text him now?"

"Might as well," I put her on speaker, so that I can type and talk at the same time. "Done."

"Great, are you going to go to bed now?"

"I'm a little too keyed up, to be honest. I think I'll get a snack and then see how I'm feeling."

"Okay, ma chère. Enjoy. I love you."

"Love you too!"

I get off my bed and head to the kitchen. Maybe I'll make myself a cup of hot chocolate. I go to turn on the kitchen light and then see a figure in the darkness.

"Ah!"

"Relax, Nin. It's only me." I flip the light and see Roderick sitting at the breakfast bar.

"You scared me! What were you doing just sitting in the dark?"

"Just thinking and praying." When I get closer to him, I see his eyes are bloodshot.

"Hey, have you been crying, Rick?"

His answer, "Yeah", hangs heavy with sadness in the air.

"Do you want to tell me what's wrong?"

"Well, it's about you, Ruthia. You and me."

"Oh?" Where is this going?

"So, you know how I'm reading 1 Samuel."

I nod. "Yeah, you went Old Testament after reading through Luke."

"Well, the relationship between David and Jonathan came up. It's hard to tell whether it's romantic or platonic, so I did some digging online."

I'm confused about how this relates to me. "Okay ...?"

"So, honestly, I don't have an answer to that question. But what came up was how Jonathan's actions toward David demonstrated he was giving the throne to David. This wasn't because Jonathan would've been an evil king, but because David is God's choice for king. It was then that I felt God speaking to me about us. He said that I'd have to give up pursuing your heart. That we could have a beautiful future together, but that I'm not his choice for you. Shane is." His voice is a mix of sadness and acceptance.

"Oh wow." I have to sit down to process his words.

"Yeah. How is what I just shared landing on you?"

"Well, I didn't tell you this, but I've been fasting for the last few weeks to seek God on what his will is for me romantically." He looks surprised. "He just told me tonight that his choice is Shane. So what you've just shared is confirmation to me."

"And what you've just said confirms it for me. I have to confess, Nin, that this is an area of my life where I want to be disobedient to God. His decision hasn't changed the feelings I have for you, the future I want with you. But I know that it's what he wants. And he's calling me to want his will more than my own."

His words stab at my heart. "I know. I feel both grief and peace at his answer. Rick, I want you to know that I would've counted it as a privilege to be the woman God has chosen for you."

I see the effect my words have on him. They lighten the shadow on his face. "Thanks, Nin. I must say, you've set a high bar for me." We exchange smiles and then he takes a deep breath. "May I pray for you and Shane?"

I'm touched by his offer. He's disappointed but fully surrendered to God's will. "Sure, thanks." We bow our heads and close our eyes.

"Heavenly Father, thank you for speaking to us through Your Spirit tonight. Lord, I ask that You bless Shane and Ruthia. That they would have you as the center of their relationship and that they would have a happy, healthy and holy life together. In Jesus's name, amen."

Tears are in my eyes as they open with the end of his prayer. I can see tears making their way down his face, too.

"Rick, I..." I don't even know what I want to say. I just wish this situation could be easier.

"It's okay, Nin. Really. I'll be alright." In his eyes, I see strength and conviction. He's going to obey God in this, regardless of how he feels.

"Well, let me give you a hug?"

He smiles at my invitation and nods. We get up, and I step into his waiting arms. His hold is firm and when he releases me, I know he's done so emotionally as well.

"I'm going to head to bed. I'll see you later."

I give him a wave and then go to prepare myself that cup of hot chocolate.

I'm measuring out the chocolate powder into a mug when I hear Rarity's voice. "Ruthia?"

I turn to see her coming from the direction of the library. It's weird that she's still up. As she comes closer, I can see her eyes are red.

"Rare, what's wrong?"

She sits at the breakfast bar and sighs. "I overheard you and Roderick."

Oh.

"Did I hurt your feelings by not being with your brother?"

She shakes her head. "No, it was just so sad because you two would be such a good fit and like each other. I just ... I don't understand why you guys can't be together." She sounds frustrated.

How would I explain this? "Well, we both feel that us being together is not something that God wants."

"And you love your God that much?"

"Yeah, we do." I can't hide the confidence in my voice.

"Why?"

"Because he's wonderful and kind and good. And he loves us more than we can even fathom. He loved me enough to die for me. Any love I have for him is but a fraction of the love he shows me." The words spill out of me.

Rarity looks thoughtful. "Do you think this same love applies to me, too?"

"I know it does."

"You sound so sure about that."

"Because I believe it. The Bible is like one big love letter to humanity. It's filled with God's love for us and how He wants to be in a relationship with us."

"Well, I might be down to see that for myself. How would I go about that?"

Oh my gosh. Oh my gosh. Oh my gosh. "We could read the Bible together, and I'll answer questions that you have along the way."

At this, she smiles. "That would be great."

Yes! "Sweet. When would you like to start?"

"How about Sunday morning? We could do it after our jog before Cynthia wakes up."

"That works!"

"Okay. Good. I'm going to bed now. Maybe we can start our jog a little later, since it's already midnight." I glance at the time on the microwave. I can't believe that so much time has passed.

"Alright, good night!" I say to her and she waves goodbye.

"God. Thank You for opening Rarity's heart to You. May she seek You and find You and join the family of faith. Amen."

Now, time to get that cup of hot chocolate.

Chapter 20

I wake up to see a text from Shane.

Shane Reid
5:49 am
I'd love to see you too. Do you want to meet to talk about something in particular?

How should I reply? I decide to drop as many hints as possible.
Me
6:24 am
Yes. Us. ♥

Suddenly, I'm getting a phone call from him. I pick up.

"Hey, just checking to see if you meant to send that heart or if it was a slip of the finger?" He cuts to the chase super-fast.

"I meant to send it."

"And what does that mean?" I can hear the hope that he's trying to hide in his voice.

"It means…" How do I say this? And then it comes to me. "Your feelings are not unreciprocated."

Will he remember that this is what I said when we first got together? His laugh seems to suggest so.

"Well, then. Would you like to spend time together tomorrow? We could go to church together and then hang out."

That makes the most sense. I don't think it would be best for me to go with Rick to church for a little while. But, I wish he wanted to spend time with me today. I guess he's just busy?

"Sure."

"Sweet. Love you, bye!" I stare at the phone in my hands. He seemed happy about the vibe that I was sending, but he didn't even want to stay on the phone with me? What was that about? Did I make a mistake?

'Just trust Me.'

I relax when I hear God's voice. He's right, I'm getting all insecure instead of just trusting God with this relationship. He told me to be in it. He's got it all covered, even if our getting back together has had a confusing start.

The day passes by in a blur: morning jog with Rare, IHOP with Gaelle, and spending time with my mom who insisted on treating us to get our nails done. By the time I get back to the apartment, I'm wiped out and go to bed early - but excited.

I get to see Shane tomorrow.

It's weird - in a good way - to be feeling this joyful anticipation at being around him again instead of confusion and apprehension. I've been so used to shutting my heart off and quieting the part of me that loves him, but now it can express itself again and that feels freeing.

I go to bed grateful and wake up ready for our

first official time being together after getting back together. When he texts me to say that he's at the front of Rarity's building, I'm racing to get to him. There's this urgency to see him I cannot explain.

And there he is.

Leaning against the passenger door of his car. He smiles as soon as he sees me and when I step into his open arms, it feels like something in me has clicked in place. I love this man. I'm going to become a family with him soon. The last several weeks have been rough for us, but we're stronger for it.

When we break apart from the hug, we just stand there holding hands and staring at each other, taking the other in.

"Gosh, Thia, you're gorgeous. In every way. I've missed you. I love you."

My heart warms at these words.

"Same to everything you just said." That's all I manage to say before he kisses me. It's firm but quick. Good thing too, because my body was ready to respond to him in a way that wasn't appropriate for the outside of an apartment building.

"We should get going. Here, let me get the door for you." I smile at the gentlemanly gesture and duck into the car. And just like that, we're off. We barely talk on the way, but he keeps one hand on my knee, his thumb brushing my skin. The intimacy of that light and ordinary touch is not lost on me. It doesn't need words.

The service at Oasis Christian Fellowship is wonderful. I had never visited because of all the drama from the church split,, but it is great to be there. It looks like any animosity toward my dad hasn't transferred to me. Many seem so proud of my graduation and comment on how much I have grown in the last few years. It feels like being welcomed back into a family I didn't even know I had been missing. I feel the same with the musical worship. I hadn't realized how much I had missed Caribbean worship songs and how long we allow for singing until I am in it again.

And then there are the outfits! We Caribbean people love to dress up for church. We strive for excellence because God, our King, deserves nothing less. I'm so glad that my mom had packed some fancier clothes for me. My light blue pencil skirt and white lace blouse are just right. Not the fanciest person by far, but not too casual either.

It is also incredible to go through a worship service with Shane. We haven't done that together since high school. It feels so right to be singing with him and to be taking notes together during the sermon. He also looks pretty great in tan khakis, a white button-down, and a light blue bowtie. He'd texted me to ask what colour scheme I was planning for the day and coordinated. It reminds me of seeing my parents get ready together and always showing up in complementary outfits for church. It makes me feel like we are officially together because anyone who sees us could guess that we are a couple.

Lunch with his parents afterward is great. We hustle our way to Mandarin for the last hour of the lunch buffet. It's nice to catch up with his parents and to hear their encouragement regarding the pregnancy.

"I had a horrible pregnancy with Shane." his mom says. "I had severe vomiting and lost more weight than I gained."

His dad nods. "Yeah, it was a scary time. It's hard for a husband who wants to care for his wife and take care of all her problems, but not be able to fix them. All I could say for sure was that I wouldn't put her through that again. That's why you're an only child, Shane."

He looks surprised to hear that. "I had no idea."

"We never wanted you to feel guilty or like you were a burden. You are one of God's greatest gifts to us and more than worth all the struggle." His mom assures him. "But anyway, I'm glad that you've been having such a good pregnancy so far. You have the glow that people talk about."

I feel my face warm. "Oh, thank you! I appreciate that. It's weird though because I don't feel pregnant yet. It was startling to put on my skirt this morning and have it be more snug than normal."

"Well, I'm sure your mom has already offered this, but I would love to go shopping with you for maternity clothes, whenever you'd like."

I'm touched by her offer. "That would be so great! Maybe it's something the three of us can do together."

The conversation continues to flow easily. When it's time for us to leave, I'm disappointed. I want to spend more time with them. But once the waiter brings us the warm white hand towels to clean our hands, we know they want us to get out. His parents pay the bill for us and leave a tip that makes up for how long we've stayed at the table.

"Before we leave, there's something we wanted to say." His mom says and then nods to his dad.

"Yes, Ruthia. We think you're a wonderful young woman, and we want to let you know we consider you to be family." At this, he starts to tear up and pauses for a moment. "You're the daughter we always wanted but never had.".

Now, I'm crying My heart needed to be a father's daughter again.

"I don't have words to express how much what you just said means to me." My words come out in a jumble, but it looks like I'm understood, anyway. They both stand with their arms extended for a hug, and I walk right into their embrace. I feel so loved by them. This makes me even more reluctant to leave them.

"Maybe we can spend some more time together this afternoon? Watch a movie or something?"

His parents exchange a look at my suggestion. I'm trying to decipher what it means when Shane says, "You know what? I'd be down for that. But, there's something that I need to get from my apartment. We can go there afterwards."

"Sounds good." We leave the restaurant and drive over to his apartment building. When we pull into the visitor's parking lot, I assume that I'm staying in the car to wait for him, but he comes over to my door and opens it for me.

"Maybe I should stay in the car? It may not be wise for us to be alone in your apartment together. It kind of violates that privacy in public principle that Corin and Zara gave us."

He thinks for a moment. "You're right. I have a surprise for you, though, and you need to come into the apartment building for it."

"Okay, I'll come. But we have to be quick."

He smiles his thanks and offers me his hand to get out of the car. He continues to hold my hand as we go through the entrance. I go to make the right turn to his apartment on the ground floor, but he stops me.

"We're going to need to use the elevator for the surprise."

I raise my eyebrow at him. "It's the suspense for me."

He laughs, pressing the up button. Once we're in the elevator, he presses the number seven.

"Do you know someone on this floor that you want me to meet or something?"

"Or something." His eyes tell me he's enjoying being vague and keeping me on his toes.

When we get to the floor, he guides us to make a left and then stops at apartment 709. When he takes out a key for the door, I'm even more surprised.

"Where exactly are we?"

"Our new apartment."

I stare at him in shock. "What do you mean?"

"I mean, I signed a lease for this apartment a week ago. It's mine. Well, ours."

"A week ago?" I'm stupefied and unable to move.

"Yes. Go in, take a look."

I nod. As I walk in, I'm met with a coat closet. To the right, there's a dining room area and a few stairs leading to a large living room. Windows make up one of the living room walls and they open to a balcony. I walk a bit more in that direction and see that the kitchen is right beside the dining area.

"Hey Thia, come over to this side." Shane

beckons me to the left. I follow him and he points out a small but reasonable bedroom on our right. "I picture this being the nursery."

All I can do is nod. We walk a few more steps, and he points out a laundry room. At the end of the hallway is a full bathroom.

"And for the grand finale: the master bedroom." He opens the door, and I gasp.

It's a large space with balcony access as well. But what undoes me is a blue blanket on the floor surrounded by candles and fairy lights.

Without me noticing, Shane has walked in and is kneeling in the center of the blanket.

He's holding a chocolate brown ring box that holds a round solitaire diamond ring. "Ruthia Walkins. I love you. I love your love for God, your kindness, your sense of humor, your care for children, and so much more. There's no one else I would rather be the mother to my child, and hopefully, children. There's no one else I would want to have my last name other than you. I know that I've made mistakes, but we've come back from them. We are an example of what reconciliation can look like. While our present circumstances were unplanned, they've only sped up where I would like to be for the rest of my life. It's only been a detour on the road of our life together. So, Ruthia Nicole Sapphire Walkins, would you do me the honor of becoming Ruthia Nicole Sapphire Reid by marrying me?"

His words fill me until it feels like I could burst with happiness and love. "Yes." It comes out as a whisper, so I clear my throat and try again. "Yes, Shane Reid, I will marry you."

With steady fingers, he slips the ring onto the third finger of my left hand. When he stands, I expect a hug or a kiss but instead, he yells. "SHE SAID YES." Immediately, the closet door opens, and Gaelle comes running out.

We jump and hug and squeal like crazy together as she yells repeatedly. "My best friend is a fiancée! My best friend is a fiancée!"

When we've calmed down, I notice Az there as well, giving Shane a hug. "Congrats, man."

Then Shane walks over toward me and pulls me into a hug. He holds me tightly and whispers, "I can't wait to start our life together."

Epilogue

"You're already 3 and a half centimetres dilated, so I think all we'll have to do is break your water and you'll go into labour pretty quickly." Dr. Parks says to me at the foot of the hospital bed.

"Okay. Let's do this!"

She laughs at my enthusiasm and starts talking to one of the nurses.

I glance at Shane, sitting on a chair to the left of me. He looks more nervous than I do.

"It's all going to be okay." I grab his hand with my left one. The light hits my ring in a way that makes a mini rainbow.

"So, Ruthia, I'm going to put this inside of you," she directs my attention to a stick in her hand. It looks like what would happen if a Q-tip and a popsicle stick had a baby. "And we're going to use it to pop open your amniotic sac."

I nod and feel a bit of pressure as her hand goes inside. Then I feel a burst, and it feels like I've wet myself.

"All done. If I remember correctly from your birth plan, you wanted an epidural, right?"

"Yep."

"Okay, I'll send the anesthesiologist in to see you and administer that. Once they do that, I'll have the nurses put you on Pitocin. That'll make labour progress faster."

I appreciate all the information that she gives me. It makes me feel less anxious. Honestly, she has managed my anxiety well throughout this entire process. Like, she knew the uncertainty of when the baby would come was amplifying my anxiety, so she asked if I'd want to schedule an induction. And here we are on the evening of the last Friday of November.

"Sounds good, Dr. Parks."

"Remember, you can call me Sandra." She reminds me, and I smile.

It's not long before the anesthesiologist comes in for the epidural. He has me sit on the bed and bend over slightly.

I'm getting anxious about this. Shane must tell from the look on my face. He squats in front of me and holds my hands.

"You're a superstar, and you can handle this. You're safe. It's all going to be okay."

I nod at him and try to keep my breathing even.

I appreciate that he's quick with his work. Pretty soon, I'm back lying down on the bed with an IV and the epidural in place.

"How are you feeling? Are you comfortable?" Shane is flustered in trying to care for me.

"I'm good. It just feels like I'm cramping on my period. It's not too bad."

"So, you're happy with your choice?"

I had been going back and forth about whether I

wanted an unmedicated birth. I believe that birth is a powerful process, not a medical one. But I have a horrible pain tolerance, and I didn't want to be traumatized by my birthing experience. "Yeah, I am. This feels more restful and less stressful so far."

"Good."

Then his phone buzzes. He glances at the screen. "It's our wedding photographer and videographer. Should I pick up?"

"Yeah, go for it!" Could our photos and video be ready? It's been about 7 weeks of waiting.

"Hey. In my email? Great! Thanks."

He smiles at me. "They're ready!"

He opens his email and sure enough, there's one from our photographer with a Dropbox link. We click through and there are our photos and a video.

"Let's do the video first," I suggest.

He nods and taps it. It's a beautiful montage of our wedding. From us getting ready with our people to my mom walking me down the aisle to our first dance. I begin to tear up remembering that day. It's one of the few days of my life that I can confidently say that I felt no anxiety.

"I love your dress." A nurse comments as she adjusts my IV. I hadn't even realized she was there.

"Thank you!" I have to agree. An ivory, strapless sweetheart ball gown that is edged around in lace. You can't even tell that I'm pregnant in the dress, which is one reason I chose it.

Once we're done watching the video, we click through the pictures. The fall colors of October are in all their glory and it's breathtaking. The Alderlea house was the right choice for our wedding and reception. It was small, but all the people we wanted there were present and that's what matters.

We spend some time reminiscing about the day when Dr. Parks comes back. "Hey, I'm just poking my head in to let you know that this may take a little while, so you can even try to sleep. It will help you save your energy for pushing when the time comes."

"Okay. Thank you!"

I check the time and see that it's almost 10 pm. "Truthfully, I feel too excited to go to sleep, but I'm going to try. I'll have my headphones playing my Abide sleep meditation to see if that'll help."

"Alright. Sounds good. I'll be right here."

I smile at him and then put my headphones in.

I wake up because of an intense pain in my butt. It's about 3 in the morning. I press the button to administer more of the epidural, but it does nothing for the pain.

"Owwwww." I groan, catching Shane's attention. He comes to me with a worried look on his face.

"Are you okay?"

"It hurts!" I reach for his hand and squeeze it tightly, but he doesn't complain.

"I'll press the button to contact the nurse."

I barely hear him because of the pain. Soon a nurse is in the room. The pain fades, and it feels like I can breathe again. I tell her about the pain I've been experiencing. "That means the baby may be ready to come! It seems like your body is starting to push them out. I'll go get Dr. Parks to check you."

I nod, and then the pain returns. I groan again.

When Dr. Parks arrives, she makes quick work of checking me. "Yep, you're 10 cm dilated, and I can see your baby's head. It's time to push."

I try to remember what I've been practicing for the last few weeks. Release my pelvis and tuck in my tummy.

"Yes! Great job!"

I squeeze Shane's hand tighter and keep pushing. I feel a pressure and then a release. Then I hear a cry.

I lean back, exhausted. "Do you want to hold her and take her to Ruthia?" Dr. Parks asks Shane. He nods in awe and takes the blanketed baby. When he brings her over to me, I can see that she's covered in some blood and a creamy white substance.

She's beautiful.

He hands her to me, and I hold her close to my chest. She stops crying.

"You were amazing. She's amazing. This is all amazing." I laugh at Shane's inability to form more words.

"Yeah, she is. Our beautiful Dielle Cynthia Reid."

The End

Dear Reader,

You made it! I have gleaned from early readers that while this is not a long book, it is intense. Congrats on making it to the end!

Many themes and aspects of the Christian life are portayed in this story. Some, you may have just been introduced to for the first time. Or you may have been challenged in your personal beliefs and convictions. At different points in reading this story, you may have been triggered, experiencing discomfort, anger, sadness, or anxiety. Anything that came up for you ought to be welcomed with contemplation and curiosity towards God.

I have also provided reflection questions for you that can be found right after this note. My heart with these questions is to help you to not simply consume this book, but allow God to bring you to deeper levels of intimacy with Him, yourself, and, maybe, others. You may engage with these questions in a book club or personally with a digital or physical journal. Either way, I hope they are beneficial to your growth and development!

Lastly, I want you to know that I want to hear from you! Please leave a review to let me know the impact this story has had on you. If you have residual questions or wrestlings from The Detour, please email me, connect with me on social media or join my

reader community on our app, Gospel Love Stories. I
am so down to interact with you!

Grace and peace,
Sana'

Reflection Questions:

1. What is your understanding of and emotions towards the topic of sex outside of marriage?

2. How would you have managed Shane's rejection if you were in Ruthia's place? What is your relationship to rejection, in general?

3. How did God speak to Ruthia? How does God speak in your life? (Who does He use? What are the ways? Directly or indirectly?)

4. How do you think your parents would respond if you were in a similar situation to Ruthia? How would you respond as a parent?

5. How have you encountered spiritual warfare in your life and what was your response? How did this story contribute to your journey of understanding and navigating spiritual warfare?

6. In what ways are you being called to sacrificially support someone the way Rarity did for Ruthia?

7. Do you have a testimony or a story of spiritual transformation similar to what Ruthia and Roderick shared?

8. Is lying, even a "Rahab lie", ever appropriate? Why or why not?

9. Would you give Shane another chance? Why or why not?

10. What aspect of the mother-daughter discourse resonated with, encouraged or challenged you?

11. What is your personal opinion on whether

you can or should be romantically interested in multiple people at the same time?

12. Ruthia forgave Shane, but she doesn't trust him. How is trust earned?

13. Did Roderick and Ruthia cross any boundaries before they expressed mutual interest? What are your personal boundaries for male-female friendships?

14. What is your experience with prayer and fasting? Would you have fasted and prayed to discern who to be with, like Ruthia did?

15. The Hawt Messies call was a safe space for the women to be vulnerable. Do you have this kind of space in your life? Why or why not? Why is living in vulnerable community so necessary to the Christian life?

16. Why was Shane's visit to her parents so pivotal?

17. How did you feel about the pre-engagement questions?

18. Were you #TeamShane or #TeamRoderick? How do you feel about the choice of Shane?

19. How was Shane an idol in Ruthia's life? Who or what are the idols in your life?

20. God told Roderick that he was not His choice for Ruthia. When has God told you no to something you wanted? How did you respond?

21. How did Ruthia and Roderick contribute to Rarity's spiritual journey? How are you doing the same with non Christians in your life?

Sana' Watts is a follower of Jesus who enjoys joining the ultimate Creator in creating worlds with her words. She is passionate about the intersection of faith and mental health as well as coming alongside people in their faith journeys. Sana' is currently pursuing a Master's of Psychospiritual Studies at Knox College with a specialisation in Spiritual Care and Psychotherapy. She is the award-winning author of Fragile and Flourishing and enjoys writing poetry and reflections upon faith in her life. Sana' is happily the wife of Desmond and mother to two children. She currently attends Church of the City Brampton and loves her city.

www.ingramcontent.com/pod-product-compliance
Lightning Source LLC
Chambersburg PA
CBHW060300310726
48976CB00007B/2153